The Basement Office

E. SABBAG

Triumph Ventures, Inc.
www.TriumphCharters.com/books.html

DEDICATION

To my editor and most relentless critic, my husband Doug, without whom this book would not exist.

The Basement Office

Prologue

The foreman, John Walls, surprises everyone by swearing at the carpenters. The youngest one flips him off before returning to the framing. The kid isn't to blame; John has been a bastard to work for lately. Instead of retaliating, he sighs and rubs the sweat off his forehead with the back of his hand.

So far, nothing has gone right on this house. It's two months behind and slipping more every day. He won't be surprised if the general contractor fires him and puts in someone who can handle it. That thought brings on a fresh bout of heartburn and he pops two more Tums, jaws grinding as he slowly chews. Jesus, here I am, forty-two, and already can't handle a chili dog. I'll be on oatmeal and Egg Beaters before you know it.

"John," declares the senior electrician "we got big problems."

"What now?" John snaps, grateful for a distraction, but dreading another crisis.

"There's water in the basement and it's shorting out the wiring."

"Damn," John swears and shoves the man aside. He grabs a flashlight before stomping down the stairs into the basement. Everyone else remains upstairs, not wanting to cross him when he's on edge. Lately, he's always on edge, with his twin daughters in college and his wife wanting a hot tub, a Lexis, vacations in Hawaii, whatever. He's just a foreman for god's sake, not the frigging contractor.

He swings the light around and surveys the damage. His indigestion burns, making him wish he'd chosen oatmeal instead of the Chicago Special. Or at least skipped the jalapeños. As the light breaks up the gloom, an inky shape flicks out of sight around a corner. John frowns while creeping towards the movement, praying that it isn't a rat.

"That's all I need," he mutters. Nothing screws up a job site faster than rats. He pushes some trash aside and reveals the crimson glow of multiple eyes. Focused on him. Bearing down on him. His last thought before the creatures fly at him, all glistening fangs and outstretched claws, is that it isn't heartburn after all. He clutches his chest and crumples beneath the onset.

1.

Alan Wilcox grits his teeth as the aquamarine sedan drifts into his lane. He clenches his fist to lay on the horn, but the letters 'AIRBAG' stop him. Furious, he fumbles for the button on the side of the wheel and presses it with his thumb. The resulting 'bleep' is more embarrassing than satisfying and only adds to his rage. The sedan, oblivious of the fury behind it, plods along, limiting Alan's speed to the point where it's impossible to pass. Alan refocuses his anger on the candy-assed state legislature that outlaws the transportation of loaded guns and settles in for a frustrating drive home.

Usually he enjoys freeway tag, outmaneuvering his foes with the precision of a fighter pilot, but today that thrill is grounded. And, although Grandma Moses is holding her vehicle to a sedate fifty miles an hour in the fast lane, she isn't the real source of his anger. No, it had started much earlier. As the cars on the right whip by, Alan sighs and drifts back to that morning.

"It's a great concept, isn't it?" Steve crows. The group that hovers around him like a cloud of flies, bobs their heads in agreement. If he'd said, 'this is a steaming crock of shit, isn't it?' they'd have agreed just as eagerly. Alan, never one to follow the crowd - probably the main reason his career and his drive home are going nowhere fast - scowls.

"What's wrong Wilcox? Not your cup of tea?" somebody smirks.

"Yeah, and a nice cuppa tea is important to you guys, isn't it?" sniggers another member of the young, clean-shaven entourage. Alan isn't sure of his name, but it doesn't matter. They dress alike, think alike, and could even be connected through some weird cyber-net that allows them to communicate on a different plane of consciousness. At least different from the one Alan is on. Access is denied once you hit forty. Around him, the banter eddies, triggered internally through their cyber-net connection. Steve smiles in a way that could be directed towards the boys or towards Alan. A perfect balancing act.

Alan assumes his fighting stance and empty eyes swivel toward him. "This whole idea sucks," he declares. The cyber-youth frown; some mutter.

Steve's smile kicks up a notch. The same dazzling smile that had carried him through one of the toughest engineering schools in the nation. True, he'd barely made it, but afterwards that smile had catapulted Steve into a cushy management position. Alan's jaw clenches as an inner voice whispers, "*and who made that happen? Who was his tutor? His champion? Hmmm?*" Alan pushes the voice away and focuses on Steve's predictable rebuttal.

"Alan, tearing down cubicle walls, opening up the work area —this approach has proven invaluable for enhancing open communication and productivity. Once you get used to it, you'll wonder why you were ever upset about it."

"I notice you haven't given up your office with the view," Alan shoots back. A flicker of triumph flashes as Alan notes the almost imperceptible wince that passes over Steve's perfect, tanned brow. Good thing he'd been paying attention, because it disappears as quickly as it appears.

"There are certain needs demanded by my position that require privacy. If you had my responsibilities, you'd understand."

Infuriated by the personal jab, Alan spins on one heel and strides away, ignoring the rippling laughter that follows him down the hall. The remainder of the day he spends sequestered away from human contact, stewing over the upcoming reorganization.

Brake lights suddenly flash in spite of the clear highway ahead and he stomps on the brakes, throwing his generous belly into the steering wheel and his car into a swerve. He gets the vehicle back under control but for this crime, he doesn't bother with the pathetic horn. Instead he shouts the required epithets punctuated with the standard hand gesture. The cursed driver, now thoughtlessly engrossed in a cell phone conversation, doesn't even look up. By the time Alan pulls off the expressway, his rage has achieved critical mass.

The idiocy of his fellow commuters—no, it isn't accurate to select just a subset. Make that fellow human beings—isn't the only irritant that day. The heat has been oppressive, even for July, and there isn't any relief on the horizon. The fledgling neighborhood's new asphalt shimmers in the sunshine, bereft of the shade provided by mature trees. What isn't bare lots or skeletal construction is brand new houses, surrounded by twig-like saplings that are struggling to survive against the relentless drought. Even so, thinks Alan, as he passes block after block of crisp brown lawns, at least this neighborhood only needs water. The signs of suburban growth fade until they're gone as he reaches the turn off to his house. Heat, sun crisped vegetation, and pathetic 'Lots for Sale' signs are everywhere. There isn't a house in sight except for his, crouched like a spider at the end of the cul-de-sac.

The car slows of its own volition as he rolls down the final stretch. Alan scowls at the elegant monstrosity that is sucking his wallet dry. *It's beautiful, but who cares?* The condo had been fine, as had been the comfortable old furniture that Lisa had insisted they'd grown out of.

In spite of the constant worry about money, for the first time that day Alan feels the tightness in his jaw release. No matter how bad life seems, there is always Lisa. A tiny smile plays on his lips as Alan eases the car's speed back up. The house loses its cloak of menace, though still wrapped in lonely desolation.

Alan slips through the house, hoping to surprise his wife. Sweat beads on his forehead, the air conditioner not quite keeping pace with the heat outside. He can just make out her head above the back of the sofa. He sneaks up behind her and places a resounding kiss on her shining black hair. She jumps, body twisting around, hazel eyes wide behind black-rimmed glasses. Mouth hanging open, Alan gasps. "My God. What happened to you?"

Square chin jutting out in defiance, Lisa says, "I got my hair cut."

"I can see that. You know I like your hair long."

"Yes, yes, I know. That's why I didn't tell you," she says. The words tumbling over each other as she hurries to explain. To justify. "Look, I've had the same hairstyle for ten years. I needed a change." Her eyes dart back and forth, seeking understanding or at least tolerance, but Alan refuses to oblige. She drops her eyes and mutters, "You know, something more sophisticated, more—suitable for my—umm—position." Her voice trails away, dragging her initial conviction along with it.

Buried in too shallow a grave, Alan's rage erupts. "That's just great. Looking like a guy is a requirement for being a manager? What's next, a sex change? Don't worry about buying the equipment, you can have mine." While the angry words crackle and spit in the sullen, humid air, Alan stalks out of the room.

In the resulting silence, Lisa bites her lower lip, fighting to hold back the tears. The coppery taste of blood fills her mouth. Looking out through the sun-baked afternoon, she wishes, not for the first or even the hundredth time, that they had neighbors, or at least one neighbor, to lend a sympathetic shoulder to cry on. Out of the corner of her eye, she sees a gray shadow slinking into the room.

"Gandalf," she murmurs in a shaky voice as she holds out a hand to the cat. His eyes glow, pieces of emerald coal. He contemplates her outstretched hand with disdain. "Here, kitty, kitty..." The big gray and white tomcat yawns and turns away, either insulted by the diminutive title or just not in a mood to socialize. In spite of her calls, he turns and stalks out of the room. "Fine," Lisa snaps, "I don't need you or Alan or neighbors."

A new record is set, worthy of Guinness. Lisa manages to hold out almost an hour before tracking down her husband.

Since he isn't out on the deck, the next option is the basement. She moves through the house, somehow unnerved by the gloom that has settled into the lifeless rooms. The kitchen is the worst, murky with melancholy light that slows her journey to a crawl. She finally arrives at the door that leads to the basement. Lisa takes a deep breath then wrenches the door open and begins her descent. Her legs are wooden, balking at the movement, but she forces them to continue, refusing to give in to silly fears. Halfway down the stairs, a malodorous breeze whispers past her cheek. She hesitates, lifting a hand to her face. As quickly as it appears, the fetid draft fades away. Shivering, Lisa hurries on.

To the right of the stairs, Alan had set up a workbench to indulge in remote control vehicles. The rest of the basement is empty except for a few boxes that Lisa plans to sort through when she has time. A time that never arrives. And so the boxes sit, their contents mostly forgotten. Now they are completely ignored as Lisa sees Alan hunched over his latest project, some kind of remote controlled plane. A fluorescent light buzzes from the ceiling, illuminating the bench and not much else. Off to the left, large shapes crouch. They should be the furnace and the water heater, but hidden in the shadows, they could be anything.

"Alan?" she ventures, her voice clanging against bleak gray walls. The bent figure doesn't move. Doesn't acknowledge her existence. Her intrusion. Lisa stands for a few seconds then crosses the floor to his workbench. "Can I get you a beer? Something to eat?"

"I'm fine," Alan barks, never looking up from his soldering. His concentration mimicking that of a doctor performing critical surgery.

Lisa squeezes her eyes against the threatening tears and tries another tack. Her voice light, conversational, she says, "Have you noticed a musty smell down here? I think there may be a leak in the foundation."

The comment gets a response, but not what she hoped for. Alan twists around on his stool and glares, his eyes blazing and cold. Ice cold. Looking at her but not seeing her. "Wonderful. We blow our life savings on a dump that doesn't hold up for even a year. Great. Just great," he snaps and returns to his tinkering.

Tears flow without interference as Lisa runs back up the stairs, unmindful of anything but the agony that rips through her body.

Lisa doesn't want to look at the clock when the bedsprings finally groan, announcing Alan's arrival. If she did, then she'd know how long she'd been crying and that is information she doesn't need. She lies still, not even allowing her breath to give her away, waiting for him to situate himself. When movement ceases, she rolls on her side, facing his back and slides her arms around his chest. She winces as she feels him tense.

"The haircut wasn't to hurt you," she whispers. Long seconds pass. She begins to think he will ignore her again. That this night will be another interminable gulf between them. But finally he sighs and rolls over, his body relaxing into hers.

"Don't worry about it. I'll get used to it. Just like everything else."

Lisa isn't sure what the 'everything else' is, but for now it's unimportant. What she wants—needs—is to get past this furious stranger. She presses her lips against his, parting them slightly in invitation. At first Alan resists, his body rigid, but then he gives in, his arms encasing her in a familiar embrace.

On a level untouched by the relief that flows through her body, she notes that he must have gotten his own beer since the dense smell coats his breath. Lisa inhales the fragrance that clings to him, a mixture of beer, deodorant and a sweet whiff of fabric softener, and sighs, content now that her husband is back. She feels his need hardening against her and she slips out of her flowered cotton briefs. In almost the same movement, he sheds his briefs and suddenly there is skin against skin. A breeze flows from the open window and Lisa shivers.

"Cold?" asks Alan, his voice rough, urgent.

"I'm fine," she murmurs and draws him to her once again. His lips slide over her neck and down to her breasts and he begins to nuzzle them gently. It feels nice, it always feels nice, but a glance at the clock reveals how very late it is. Lisa grasps him with her hand and begins to rub. A moan escapes from the lips at her chest; the buzzing tickles her. She fights to stifle her laughter and guides him inside her, using her fingers to spread the soft folds. It is difficult at first, she is still dry, but he is patient, waiting for her to ease the way.

When Alan is completely inside her, he settles into a rhythm. Closing her eyes Lisa arches her back and begins to move with him, matching his little grunts with moans of her own. His thrusts come faster, but not fast enough. Lisa speeds up, wrapping her legs around him while raking her nails gently down his back. This does the trick. With one last thrust, she feels him pumping, exploding, emptying. Exhausted by her performance, she lays back against the pillows and smiles as Alan rolls off her and onto his side of the bed.

Lisa smoothes the dark, thinning hair away from his sweat-covered brow and murmurs, "Everything better?"

His teeth flash white in the dark room. "Yeah. Everything's better."

"Good. Sleep tight sweetheart."

"You too," he answers, his voice now thick and drowsy. "Lisa?"

"Mmmm?"

"Love you. More than anything."

"Same here. Go to sleep." His breathing becomes slow and even as Lisa stares at the ceiling. Tomorrow is going to come very early, but for now, the warmth spreading down her thighs fills her with contentment. "Maybe this time," she whispers. "Maybe this time…"

2.

As Lisa pounds away at the merciless treadmill, she passes the time by listing the things she hates most in the world. One: Working out. Two: Shapely young body builders that don't truly appreciate their shapely young bodies. Three: Floor to ceiling mirrors that reflect shapeless, not so young, bodies. It's bad enough that she's forced to spend a gorgeous Saturday morning here when she could be lounging on the deck watching clouds drift by. There's no need to constantly remind her that her waist of twenty is gone forever. Furious, she sticks out her tongue at the red-faced image, huffing and puffing away in the mirror. Seeing that wretched person reminds her that the honor of top hate is given to the sadistic torture devices masquerading as exercise machines. *And to think I pay for this.*

As her thoughts and legs march to the rhythm of the treadmill, she glances around the gym. A tall, lean redhead with a spectacular body clad in an appropriately spectacular green leotard is sauntering across the floor, coolly acknowledging the worship that follows her progress. Lisa looks down at her ratty gray sweats and searches desperately for something to hide behind, but it's too late. Beth Wright sees her prey and zeros in. Lisa groans.

"Hi! Glorious day for a workout, isn't it?" the young beauty chirps, as she leaps onto the treadmill alongside Lisa's. Within seconds, the red head's machine whizzes along at an impossible angle. Lisa tweaks her machine to match and is immediately sorry.

"If you say so," Lisa gasps.

Beth smiles a toothy grin that would make any crocodile envious, and any antelope cower in terror. "I'm impressed. Most women your age have already given up," she says as she flies along at about Mach 10. "I only hope I have your determination when I get to be as old as you."

Lisa throws a homicidal look over her shoulder and bites her lip. "Thanks," she mutters. The old adage about old age and treachery winning out over youth and enthusiasm flashes through her mind. Sadly, the latter definitely have the upper hand at this moment.

Beth dabs at tiny pearls of sweat glistening on her forehead, her lips parted slightly. Two body builders stroll by, undisguised admiration beaming as they scan Beth. Their eyes slide over Lisa the same way one examines drywall. She hunches her shoulders and grips the bar as if her life depends on it. Of course, right now, it does.

"So," Beth says, the syllable causing Lisa to jump. "Alan and Steve are pretty tight, aren't they?"

"All three of us are." The statement is curt, but conserving energy is now a necessary survival tactic. She contemplates whether Beth will notice if she passes out or just keep on talking. Mouth to mouth is out of the question; the girl probably thinks age is contagious.

"Oh, right. You guys went to college together, didn't you?"

"Yep."

"I keep forgetting Steve's your age. He seems so much younger." Dab at the forehead—dab at the neck. "I think he's just wonderful, good looks, great personality, promising future." Lisa muffles a groan as Beth turns up her machine with nary a break in the conversation. "Great in bed...." A dull flush creeps up Lisa's neck and she stubbornly increases the speed on her treadmill.

"Better not overdue it," Beth cautions with another crocodilian grin. A few seconds of blessed silence, then "Maybe the four of us should get together and do something sometime. I'd love to get to know Steve's old buddies better." She allows the treadmill to carry her backward and hops off in mid-stride. "See you later," and, with an airy toss of her auburn mane, she struts off.

"Bitch," Lisa mutters. She can turn down the treadmill, but doesn't, preferring instead to let the tortuous exercise burn away the thoughts somersaulting through her head.

Alan quickly and efficiently slices up a mushroom and adds it to the growing pile of vegetables in the wooden salad bowl. Lisa, seated on a barstool across from him, grabs one of the freshly cut slices and pops it in her mouth. Alan picks up a long-handled wooden spoon and raps her firmly across the knuckles. "Ow," she says, pulling her hand out of reach. "That hurt."

"You deserve it. Take all you want of the whole ones."

With a mischievous grin, she smirks, "Nope, not as much fun," and snatches a clump of mushrooms from the bowl. This time, she is fast enough to elude his menacing spoon.

"That's it," he growls, "keep it up and you're the cook from now on."

"Idle threat." She retorts, barely understandable above her munching. "You know that means sure starvation."

"Good point. All right, eat all you want."

"You don't have to agree so easily," she protests and throws a mushroom cap at his head. He dodges the missile and it flies past his ear, rolling across the kitchen floor. Gandalf magically appears and pounces, pummeling it into submission. Once convinced of its surrender, the triumphant feline hurries off to the living room, the trophy clamped in his teeth. Lisa meets Alan's gaze and they laugh. The big tom has always made them laugh.

Years ago, a scrawny, mewling ball of fur had wandered onto the construction site of their new home. The workmen enjoyed feeding the kitten scraps, but none wanted a permanent responsibility. Lisa and Alan had come by to check on the progress of their house and it was love at first sight. At least it was between Lisa and the kitten. Alan resisted for a while, but in the end the pair was too much for him. Now, Alan can't imagine the house without the big gray tomcat.

Alan returns to his preparations. He finishes the salad before Lisa can pilfer anything else. "What're we having?" Lisa asks.

"Steaks, baked potatoes and rolls."

"Yum. Is Steve bringing anyone?"

"No, I tried to talk him into bringing Beth, but he thinks you don't like her."

"Smart boy," Lisa grumbles.

"You're not being fair. She's pretty nice when you get to know her."

"She's a twit."

"Why do you say that? Have you ever really tried talking to her?"

"As a matter of fact, smart guy, I had a conversation with her today."

"Where?"

"At the club. She plopped down on the treadmill next to mine. After she patronized me, insulted me, and flaunted her body, I wasn't feeling too neighborly."

Alan stops slicing. "What'd she say?"

Lisa scowls. "Nothing specific, just snide comments about my age and how wonderful that I'm trying to maintain my figure given that I'm such an ancient hag."

"Did she actually say hag or just imply it?"

"Who cares?"

Convinced he's on thin ice, Alan plows on anyway. "Don't worry, I like my women cuddly. I'll keep you around no matter how much you put on over the years...."

Lisa starts to sputter as the doorbell rings. She gives Alan one last glare before going to the door. For a few moments it's quiet, and then he hears Lisa's bright, high laughter, always more relaxed with Steve than with anyone else. *Even me.* The familiar prickle of jealousy itches at the back of his neck for a second before he pushes it away. Steve and Lisa were friends first, inviting Alan into their circle after he'd tutored both of them through freshman Calculus. Steve hopped from woman to woman while Alan fell head over heels, hopelessly in love with Lisa. She had returned the love, then and since, never giving him reason for doubt. In spite of this, his jaw clenches as he chops violently at the helpless vegetables on the cutting block.

"Behold," Steve announces as he enters the kitchen, his exuberant blond presence overwhelming the suddenly small space, "a stranger bearing gifts." With a flourish he produces a bottle of wine—an extremely expensive bottle of wine—and sets it on the counter. Comfortable from years of friendship, he heads to the refrigerator and pulls out a beer, pausing as he asks. "Lisa? Alan?"

"Yeah, thanks," Alan says as he takes the offered beer.

Lisa shakes her head. "None for me."

Steve frowns slightly before shrugging and closing the door. He takes a long drink and then says, "Smart girl. Probably outlive all of us. Alan, Lisa tells me you don't like her sexy new look. What gives? No change is good change?"

Lisa flushes and tries to get Steve's attention. Steve ignores her signals and grins at Alan. Alan continues slicing, his clenched jaw aching. It takes a few beers, the bottle of wine and a few more beers until Alan relaxes enough to enjoy the evening.

After polishing off Alan's excellent meal and convincing Steve that the dishes can wait, the trio sits on the deck and watches the sun disappear over the horizon. The evening sky is ablaze with fiery streaks of orange, gold and magenta that blend into deep, soft violet. The friends are quiet as they watch the spectacle fade into a blackness pierced by icy stars. Steve is the one that breaks silence.

"So, Alan, how's work these days? Is the revolution over or just beginning?

"I don't know. This new setup's intolerable."

Lisa shifts in her lounge chair. "At least it's good to see you're giving it a chance."

Alan glares, but doesn't respond to the jab.

Steve takes a deep swallow of his beer, studies the bottle and then peels away a corner of the label. "Have you considered alternatives?"

"Such as?"

"Working from home, for instance."

Alan leans forward, searching Steve's face for any sign of teasing. He doesn't find any, so he nods. "Sure."

"I know a lot of people think about it, but it's not right for everyone," Steve replies. "The company's been thinking about instituting a work at home program and I think you'd be ideal."

"Who's in charge of this marvelous plan?" Lisa demands, the sarcasm harsh in the soft night air.

Steve throws her a frown then turns back to Alan. "It's my idea and I think it's a great opportunity for the right person."

"This isn't the first step towards letting me go, is it?" Alan asks, his smile not quite reaching his eyes.

Steve should laugh, but doesn't. A brief smile then, "There are rumors that the company is planning some—um—rightsizing initiatives. A year ago I'd have said you'd never make the short list. But recently..." Steve shrugs. A pause, then a laugh. Hearty. Booming. False. "What am I saying? Don't be paranoid. You're one of the best engineers at Benton International. Maybe *the* best. No one wants to let you go. No one will let you go."

Alan stares at Steve. Takes a drink. Stares again. "What's the deal?"

"With the economy the way it's going, we need to cut overhead. That means leasing out some of the office space to other companies. Once that happens, there won't be as much room."

Lisa won't be left out of this conversation. She speaks up. "Is that what's driving the open bay arrangement?"

"Exactly. No partitions means you can pack more people in a smaller space." Steve continues. "Even more efficient if you move 'em off site completely."

Alan sips thoughtfully. "I guess I can buy that. Why me?"

"It's obvious. You don't want to move into management and it's obvious you hate the re-org. But you're a damn good engineer and nobody wants to lose you. You're mature, self-disciplined and, since you mostly work alone, why not do it at home?"

Alan leans forward, his face animated for the first time in weeks. "Details. I want details."

Steve launches into his pet project and Alan laps up the fervor. No one notices Lisa. She leans back, watching the two men swat the idea back and forth like a Ping Pong ball.

"Basically, you contract to do projects. You'll still be a full-time employee with all your benefits, but your pay is based on phase completion."

"A phase?"

"Yeah. You get with the project manager and develop a schedule broken up into a series of timed function blocks. Phases. At the end of each, you come into the office, have a design review to show what you've done, and then a panel decides whether or not you've completed the section. If everything's okay, you get paid."

"If not?"

"No worries. You'll know whether or not you've done your part before you come in."

"Sounds risky," Lisa observes. Both men jump at the voice emanating from the gloom.

"Maybe a little," Steve agrees, reluctantly. "But it's also exciting"

Alan nods, looking like one of those dogs with the bobbing heads. "I like it. There'd be no question as to who did the work. No more glory hounds stealing my ideas. I'd live or die by my own hand." He pauses to drink his beer and watch fireflies wink on and off. Then, struck by a new thought, he says, "What about equipment? Does the company supply that or do I need my own?"

"You should get your own."

"Why? Don't I come up short that way?"

Lisa adds, "Won't it be expensive?"

"No," Steve assures Alan, "and no," he says to Lisa, "not really. Benton will give you an interest free loan spread across two years. Since the equipment is yours, you can do whatever you want with it."

"Like what?"

"Let's say you want to do some free-lancing. Pick up a few jobs here and there. If the stuff's yours, no negative implications, legal or ethical."

"Hmmm. I like the way you think, buddy." Alan clinks his bottle against Steve's. Lisa's frown intensifies, but is lost in the darkness.

For the rest of the evening, the two men dissect and examine the idea. They discuss everything from what kind of computer to buy to how to write up the contract. It's late when Steve finally says his good-byes and leaves, but Alan chatters on, completely overlooking his wife's reticence. Eventually, he falls into an exhausted sleep, unaware that Lisa lies awake for hours more.

3.

The next morning, Alan wakes with a groan, sunlight streaming into his bloodshot eyes. The combination of too much beer and too little sleep leaves his head a pounding mess. He rolls over to ask Lisa how she feels and encounters nothing but pillows. Yawning and scratching, he stumbles out of bed and ambles through the house.

Stepping into the living room's cool dimness, curtains closed against the blazing morning sun, something squishes between his toes. He curses mildly, hopping around on one foot, trying to peel off the object. Once he pries it loose he studies it. "What the…" he trails off, grinning as the memory comes back. It's the now pitiful mushroom that Gandalf triumphantly carried off last night. Alan goes into the kitchen and tosses it in the trashcan.

Looking around, he sees a steaming pot of coffee but still no Lisa. He fixes a big mug, pours in cream and sugar, and looks out the window. Hopefully, the weatherman will make good on his promise of a break in the heat. If the drought doesn't ease up, the county is threatening a moratorium on watering. Alan scowls. Right now their verdant lawn and expensive landscaping is hanging on because of daily watering. Take that away and it becomes as barren as the surrounding vacant lots. *Great. More money down the drain.* Alan shakes away the thought and remembers last night.

No way Steve understands the kind of carrot he's dangling in front of Alan. This is the answer. The only concern now is Lisa. She'd gotten that blank, tight-lipped expression that means she's really pissed, but isn't going to say anything. When his wife gets that look, she's impossible to reason with. *Not this time*, Alan thinks, drinking his coffee. *This time she's got to understand. She's just got to. She doesn't know how bad it is.* The coffee scalds his tongue, but he doesn't notice. He gulps the burning liquid, considering his next move.

Alan knows he should hunt his wife down, and begin his

campaign, but it's nice to enjoy the peaceful morning and dream. *Where should he set up? Upstairs? The dining room? The basement?* He remembers Lisa's conviction that something is wrong downstairs. *Dampness*, he thinks. *Weird.* He'd never noticed it. He shrugs. *Could be a bargaining point.* He'll check it out, call the builder, whatever, if she'll consider Steve's plan. Satisfied with this plan of attack, Alan goes in search of his adversary.

Lisa is curled up on the swing, a wrought iron masterpiece they'd uncovered at a citywide garage sale. A steaming cup of coffee is clutched to her chest. The swing cost twenty dollars cash and countless hours to make it presentable. But now it serves as the perfect backdrop for the perfect woman. The swing engulfs Lisa, dwarfing her trim body. Soft tendrils of black hair frame her face and her huge eyes contemplate the horizon, searching for—what? A dream? The truth? An answer? A sharp pang stabs in his chest. *She's so beautiful,* he thinks as he watches her, unwilling to move, to break the spell. *So sad... My fault?* With an angry shake, he pushes the thoughts away and moves to her, easing the cup from her fingers and capturing her slender hands in his over-sized ones.

"Penny?" he asks. Her smile increases his ache.

"Nothing in particular," she says, meeting his gaze with an unflinching one of her own. Alan sits beside her, causing the bench to drift back and forth, and puts his arm around her shoulders.

"Why don't you want me working at home? Don't you trust me?" She stiffens, but he plows ahead, not waiting for an answer. "I'm dying in that place. It sucks me dry and leaves nothing. If something doesn't change, I'll explode and who knows what—or who—I'll take with me." Lisa gasps and Alan realizes that he is clenching her shoulder hard enough to drive the blood from his fingers. He releases his grasp and rubs gently instead, murmuring, "Sorry…"

Lisa twists around to look at him and parts her lips to say something. She never finishes.

It's hard to say how they wind up in the bedroom, clothes off and coupled deliciously in the still crumpled sheets, but Alan doesn't question it. He knows Lisa is upset about the extra weight she's gained, but he can't understand why. Her body has always been enticing, but now, softer, more rounded, more— voluptuous, it's incredible. The cushion of her stomach under his hips, the way her butt settles into his cupped hands, the fullness of her breasts, if he thinks about it too much he'll explode in seconds. Like a kid with his first woman. He lets his mind drift, enjoying the feel of her legs wrapped around his hips as he pumps into her, but not enjoying too much.

Is there anything else in the world that feels this good? No, in the universe. Lisa's breathing becomes deeper and her pink tongue darts out and flicks across her parched lips, leaving them shiny and inviting. Alan bends to taste her mouth, her tongue, her neck and she arches her back and moans in a purring rumble. His rhythm increases and he drives deeper, slamming into her now. He wants to feel her come, wants to know she feels as incredible as he does. He can go forever.

Suddenly, she rakes her nails down his back and gently digs into his buttocks. Control disappears. With a desperate moan Alan lets go and thrusts again and again and again. Lisa clings to him and rides it out; her breathing almost calm compared to his animalistic gasps. Sweat pours off him and settles in glistening puddles between her breasts and stomach. She gives a little laugh and he rolls away, an unexpected breeze tickling his drenched skin.

"Did you come?" he asks the ceiling.

"Mmmm…"

Alan lifts up on one elbow and says, "It's important. I want you to feel good. As good as I do."

Lisa smiles and touches his cheek. "It's fine, don't worry. I'm happy when you are."

This isn't the time, he knows it, but he blurts out before thinking. "Then let me take Steve's opportunity."

Her face chills as a muscle twitches in her jaw. Rage flickers in Alan's chest. He buries it, hoping she doesn't notice.

"I know you're having problems at work," Lisa says, each word enunciated with a drill sergeant's precision. "But changing locations isn't going to make all that go away. And there's the expense and the setup and..."

"I know all that," Alan interrupts. Impatience flares, eager to morph into anger. "But I'm also a mature professional. Or don't you believe that?" He waits for the reluctant nod, then "It's not as if I'm going to run in and announce my plans tomorrow. The whole situation needs to be analyzed and, if it looks feasible, we'll go from there. I just want to know you'll be open-minded before I put a lot of energy into the investigation."

A tear slips down his wife's cheek and Alan can feel the knots unraveling in his chest. He is ready to back down, to forget the nonsense when she says, "Okay. I can do that."

Her voice is so low it's hard to hear, but Alan doesn't question. Not now. Instead he puts his arms around her and holds her tight. Thoughts and plans and questions tumble through his head as the two lay in the sultry summer morning.

Unfortunately, crisis after crisis fills Alan's time, so it is a few days before he has a chance to price out the equipment. The resulting sum leaves Steve speechless.

"Twenty-five grand?" his friend repeats, a fork laden with salad poised halfway to his mouth.

Alan nods, his own cheeseburger (extra onions, hold the lettuce and tomato) suddenly tasteless. "That's what it comes to."

"I don't get it. You can buy a computer for a couple hundred bucks."

"Those cheap jobs can't handle my software packages, which also aren't cheap. There's at least $12K in software alone. Then, hardware design requires specialized tools. The measly two grand the company's willing to loan me doesn't even make a dent and I can't float this kind of cash. Not with the house and the furniture and everything. And forget an equity line on the house – nothing much there even if I could talk a bank into loaning me anything." Alan tosses down a few french fries and starts in on a monster cookie with chocolate chunks and macadamias.

Steve takes a healthy swig of sparkling spring water. Alan doesn't know anybody else that drinks sparkling water at lunch. "Okay, so it's more than you expected. It's an investment. You can borrow that much against your 401K."

"True," Alan agrees, "but forget about talking Lisa into using our retirement. I know because I already asked." He pauses to gather up some cookie crumbs, and then takes a bite of his cheeseburger. After swallowing, Alan continues in the same dejected tone. "She's against the idea anyway."

"You should just do it and prove she's wrong. She'll come around." There's a quiet moment, then Steve asks, "Why does she have to approve it, anyway?"

"Approve what?"

"The loan. She doesn't have to know."

Alan stares at his friend. "You don't know much about women and even less about wives. Legally, I can do it without her permission or even her knowledge. Realistically, I'd pay for it for the rest of my life. With interest."

Steve looks away and scans the cafeteria. A couple of women walk by, their laughing conversation punctuated with wild gestures, and his face contorts slightly. "Maybe that's why I'm not married. I don't need anyone's permission to succeed." He wrenches his attention back to Alan. "Are you sure you figured the cost right? Maybe you can get part of the stuff now and the rest later when you can afford it."

"Thought about it. The problem is that I need everything before I can do anything."

"That sucks. I still think this is a great opportunity, it's just a matter of making it happen."

"I know, I know," Alan agrees, "I just wish I could convince Lisa."

Steve looks at him intently. "Well, you'd better talk her into it soon or the chance may evaporate. I'm hand picking the candidates and there won't be many."

"Go ahead and pick somebody else then, 'cause I don't see

any way this is going to work." The extra onions churned in Alan's stomach.

"Look," Steve says, his tone changing from high-pressure salesman to concerned friend. "It's not *that* critical. Give it some more thought. If you change your mind, let me know."

Alan smiles. "Funny, that's the same arrangement I have with Lisa."

Ignoring a queasy feeling in the pit of his stomach, Steve heads back to his office. Turning a corner he almost runs down Phil McGinnis. Phil is a project manager who has been with Benton for twenty-seven years. He hates that Steve skyrocketed to his position in a fraction of the time that it took the older man. The office scuttlebutt is that Phil would give his left nut to see Steve taken down a notch or two. For a second, Steve smirks. The scuttlebutt also claims it is the only one Phil has left.

"Hey, Phil. What's up?"

"Not profits."

Steve grins and is pleased to see Phil's perpetual frown intensify. "Is that all you care about?"

"What else is there?"

"Nothing, I guess."

"Speaking of profitability, how's your cottage industry going?"

Just then two young women pass by and smile at Steve. He smiles back and gives a quick wave. To Phil, he says, "You mean the telecommuting program?"

"Whatever you're calling it these days."

"It looks good. I've got some solid candidates lined up for the first pass."

"Like who?"

Steve hesitates. The lunch conversation is still fresh. "Alan Wilcox."

Phil's eyebrows lift. "Alan agreed to this?"

"He's still got some details to work out, but yeah. Everything should be lined up fairly soon." Another group passes the pair in the hall, one of the men jostling Steve and everybody calling out greetings. Few are directed to Phil.

"Well," Phil snaps as he glares at the retreating backs. "I have to get back to work; I've wasted enough time. I hope for your sake this venture succeeds. Good day."

"Same to you," Steve returns. Phil pauses for a few seconds, then strides quickly towards his corner office.

Steve exhales in a rush, unaware until that moment that he's been holding his breath. He shakes himself mentally, feeling like a dog emerging from a muddy pond. The feeling persists until he runs into the cute blond temping in payroll. A few flirtatious minutes erase the unpleasant encounter from his mind.

4.

Tappa, tappa, click, click. Thump, ta-dump, dump, dump. Alan winces at the noises emanating from the neighboring desk. Without even a cubicle wall, there is no buffer between him and the idiots that pervade Benton. Alan has no idea how Dave can tap so many different objects and still produce only one sound. He glares at his oblivious neighbor, hoping the jerk is struck with a terminal case of tendonitis. Finally, Alan can't take it any longer. *A walk, some water, that'll help. Can't hurt.* Dave continues to tap, not even looking up when his neighbor stalks away.

The usual group stands by the vending machines, some waiting for coffee, most just waiting for gossip. Alan takes his time getting a drink and hears Bill, a kid half his age, accepting congratulations.

"What's up?" Alan asks.

Sue, from—sales?—maybe—pipes up. "Isn't it great? Bill was just awarded a patent."

"What for?"

Bill grins. "The infrared detector for the water heater. I still can't believe it. My first patent. It certainly took long enough."

Alan frowns. "The IR detector? Didn't I help with that?"

Bill's happy expression fades. "Well, I wouldn't say that. I've been busting my ass on it for over six months. I think you and I may have had some conversations about it, but that's all."

Everyone quits talking. Silence oozes into the vacuum.

Warmth creeps up Alan's neck. "Okay, so you implemented it, but patents are for ideas. You wouldn't have gotten anywhere without my help, buddy boy. If there's a patent on it, I deserve to share it."

Sue intervenes, her placating tone grating on Alan's bristling nerves. "Look, a lot of people contributed to the idea, but Bill put the most work into it. Besides, this is his first patent and you've got lots of 'em. Let somebody else have some attention for a change."

"Yeah, quit being such a glory hound," a voice in the back adds.

The warmth in his neck becomes nuclear. Through clenched teeth Alan snaps, "You don't get it. I'm just saying that my contributions deserve to be recognized."

Bill pushes his face into Alan's. "Are you accusing me of stealing your ideas?"

"If the shoe fits." By this time both men are shouting, the younger engineer towering over the older, his face inches from Alan's. John Clayton walks up just as the two men are about to decide the issue with their fists.

"Hey, what's going on? I can hear you two all the way out in the hall." Alan and Bill pull back and glare at each other. "Come on, Alan, I need to talk to you about some parts." John is a purchasing agent and one of Alan's closest friends. John, tall, thin, dark-haired and sporting horn-rimmed glasses bears an unfortunate resemblance to Waldo from the game 'Where's Waldo?' Today that thought not only doesn't make Alan laugh; it doesn't even cross his mind.

John grabs Alan's arm to move him away. Alan resists, but Waldo can be extremely determined when he wants to be. And there are hundreds of vendors who can attest to that fact. Alan is still fuming when they get to his desk.

"What was that all about?" John demands.

"I don't want to talk about it."

"You sure?"

"That's what I said. Now tell me what you came for or leave. I have work to do." A muscle twitches in his cheek as he and John discuss the parts order.

Alan tips a red pen end over end, mesmerized by the pattern it traces through the air. He has no idea how long the slender object transfixes him, but finally he lays the pen down, picks up the phone and dials. "Steve?   Yeah   Look, I need to talk to you—Lunch?—Sure.   See ya." He hangs up the phone and looks around. The office buzzes with energy. Dave, his face relaxed and dreamy, taps absently on a mouse pad with his Sharpie. Eventually, Alan picks up the red pen and goes to work on the layout.

The huge plate of food seems insurmountable to Lisa. After two margaritas (Alan insisted) appetizers and countless bowls of chips and salsa during the two hour wait at the bar, she's already stuffed. The best she can do is pick at her enchiladas and enjoy the alcohol induced buzz that tickles her ears. It's been a long time since she and Alan have gone out and just being here is great. She'd been apprehensive at first, Alan is not impulsive by nature, but the evening is nice. Her husband, tense and irritable for the past few – weeks? – months? – years? whatever – is relaxed and funny, the man she'd fallen in love with long ago.

"Are you going to eat that?" Alan asks as he reaches for her frijoles.

"I thought you were watching your weight," Lisa quips. When she sees the cloud pass over his smiling face, she bites her lower lip, wishing she could snatch back the words. Then the darkness fades and his smile returns, even more radiant.

"Tomorrow, I'll be good. Tonight, we celebrate."

"Celebrate?" She'd forgotten there's a motive behind the dinner. She watches Alan put away the rice and beans and braces herself.

Alan crunches into a chip and mumbles, "I'm taking Steve's offer." A single crumb clings to his lower lip, transfixing Lisa, the yellow speck waggling with every movement yet refusing to drop. Not even when he sticks out his chin. Daring her to disagree.

Lisa waits and then realizes this is the big surprise. Relieved laughter bursts out of her. Sober couples nearby frown.

"That's the big news?" Lisa can't believe it. "Why all the fanfare?"

Alan looks bewildered. "Aren't you mad?"

"It's not as if you haven't been talking about it for weeks. Besides, I said it was your decision."

"I know. I just wasn't sure you meant it."

"Of course I did. I am curious, though, why now?"

"You know that IR detector Bill Simmons was working on?"

"I think so," she says, trying to recall one project out of the hundreds Alan talks about.

"Well, he was awarded a patent for it."

"That's great," Lisa exclaims. "I'll bet he's excited. Is this his first one?"

"Yeah, but that's not the point. He didn't even tell me he was being considered for it."

Lisa frowns. "Why would he?"

Alan frowns in response. "I helped with the idea; I should get some of the recognition. And," his voice gets louder and sharper, "there's the award money. I should have gotten some of that too."

Their waiter materializes. "Can I get anything else?"

The words are sincere enough, but Lisa can tell he is praying that the answer is no. She refuses to yield. "Yes, please. How about another refill on our coffee?"

A bland smile quickly masks a flash of irritation. "But of course," he murmurs and hurries away for a pot of coffee. Alan stares into the distance, studying everything but his wife.

She sighs. "Okay, so there's this patent, but that couldn't have been it. What else?"

Alan flinches. "Not a whole lot. I confronted Bill and he got bent out of shape. Accused me of being a glory hound. I guess he felt it was his turn in the spotlight."

Secretly, Lisa disagrees with her husband. Alan has scores of patents, what's one more? She tries to picture Bill Simmons. He's a tall, bearish young man, not too long out of college. The few times she'd met him he'd seemed shy, ill at ease. She can imagine how excited he must be about his first patent and how crushed by the accusation. Careful with her tone, soothing, but not patronizing, Lisa says, "I'm sure he'll get over it. He's a big boy."

Alan shrugs. "Whatever. The silver lining was that it gave me a wake-up call. Thank god I didn't miss my chance."

Lisa feels that Steve has exaggerated the urgency, but doesn't think this is a good time to discuss that point. She tunes back in.

"… depending on how long it takes my equipment to arrive, I should be ready to start in about three or four weeks."

"Is the company handling the equipment setup?"

Alan fidgets. Stammers. "No—umm—actually I—uh—took out a loan against my retirement."

Lisa stares, wondering whether it's the alcohol or too much coffee that has distorted her hearing. "What?"

"I took out a loan. Ten years, 8.5% interest, paid back to me. It's a good deal."

"I don't care how good it is, you should have asked me first," Lisa snaps. "That isn't just *your* retirement."

"Why do I have to ask you? Be real. If I had asked you, you'd have said no. You always do." Alan's voice rises. "I'm suffocating—dying—and you don't care. Or maybe you care, but you don't believe in me. Don't trust what I can do. Well now you don't have a choice."

Maybe it's too much food. Too much alcohol. Too much coffee. Too many stares. But Lisa feels dizzy, nauseous. With a start, she realizes that the staring faces are all new and that the place is almost empty. She signals for the check and scratches out a measly tip under their waiter's baleful glare.

"Let's go," she barks, leaving without looking at her husband. Alan hesitates and then scuttles after her.

The drive home is frosty in spite of the gentle summer night. Rigidly perched in bucket seats, the earlier camaraderie has disappeared. The interminable ride drags on and on.

Once home, the two separate. Lisa heads upstairs, Alan down into the basement. Gandalf's anxious meowing is the only sound that pierces the night. Alan sits at his workbench thinking about his wife alone in their bed and hopes she's as miserable as he is. He concentrates on a particularly stubborn aileron when suddenly there's a slight scratching noise to the left. He twists around, staring into the inky shadows. Alan listens intently, but there is nothing. Only silence. He laughs but the sound is shaky. Hollow. For a second he wants to run up the stairs and away, but a vision of his waiting wife, cold and angry, stops him. He turns back to his plane and picks up the tweezers. The night rolls ponderously by, eddying around the solitary man and passing in uninterrupted silence.

5.

Jessica Baker scrutinizes her boss from across the desk. Lisa's lips move slightly as she concentrates. Jessica doesn't believe the marketing specification demands such intensity. "Well?"

Lisa's head snaps up, eyes focusing in like a camera lens. "Well, what?"

"Is it my best work yet? Go ahead. I can accept unconditional praise and adulation."

Confused, Lisa gropes for an answer from the document in front of her. Jessica laughs and takes pity. "Okay, okay, Apathy and ridicule also work. Bad, huh?"

Lisa smiles. "No, no. It's fine. I see some holes, but we can fill'em in later. My main concern about all these new projects is the lack of resources. If we aren't given the go-ahead to hire more people, we'll be two years behind instead of just one."

Jessica nods. Strong, large-framed, her hair an impossible shade of platinum, she has been a part of the marketing staff at SoftSolutions, Inc. for over fifteen years. The company name refers to their product, software solutions and services, and also a tongue in cheek reference to their female-based origins. But minority owned or not, they have been hit hard by the economy. Just like everyone else. The work is out there, the people are out there, but bringing them together means overhead. And the ongoing mandate is to cut overhead. Jessica hasn't seen anything like it since the Dot Com crash.

"All right, try this on for size. If we get more people," she notices Lisa's mouth tightening, "and we train them, and get more room and equipment, *then* is it a good idea?"

Lisa smiles. "Maybe. For you, I'll forget reality and re-examine it."

"Ouch. That hurts." Jessica clutches at her chest and falls back in her chair, Lisa just stares at the paper, eyes darting back and forth. Quietly, Jessica says, "Okay. What's going on?"

"I told you, not enough people…."

"Nope, boring; heard it a million times. What's going on with you?"

Lisa's hesitation is obvious. Jessica loves the younger woman like a sister, but their lives, and ways of looking at life, couldn't be more different. Two terminated marriages and a career, clawing her way through sales, has left Jessica flint-edged. Lisa's long marriage to her college boyfriend and a straightforward career in software development has made her a cream puff. And Jessica has never had much of a sweet tooth.

"Out with it. Now. It pisses me off to see you unhappy and, I need your support on this proposal. That means I need your focus."

"You're right," Lisa mumbles. After a second or two she adds, "It's Alan."

Jessica had made herself promise not to be judgmental, but her jaws clench. She hopes Lisa doesn't notice, but the way the little brunette straightens up in her chair and frowns confirms that she has. Jessica thinks happy thoughts. Friggin kittens and rainbows. "What about Alan? Is everything okay?"

Lisa relaxes a bit. "He's decided to work at home."

"And?" Jessica asks, a little more curtly than she wants. "What's the problem?"

"We can't afford it! And, he borrowed against his retirement money without telling me."

"Okay. I'll be the first to admit that it isn't the smartest thing he's ever done. But he is a man. And you haven't been very encouraging. Maybe he can't talk to you." Jessica watches Lisa squirm.

"All right, so I haven't been terribly supportive…" Lisa begins.

"Not supportive? You hated the idea and talked it down whenever you could."

Lisa scowls and looks down. Years drop away. She looks about twelve. "All right, all right. Maybe I did. But that doesn't change the fact that he went behind my back."

Jessica leans forward and crisscrosses her fingers into a

shelf, a perfect chin rest. "I said I agree he should've talked to you. But face facts. The loan and the interest get paid back to him, so there's no loss. You're both young, you're not retiring for years; it can't be that big a deal. What's really bothering you?"

A tear slides down Lisa's cheek. She brushes it away. "I'm just worried. He's lonely and unhappy and his health is awful. Isolation will make everything worse."

"He'll be fine," Jessica murmurs. "He's not alone. He has you." This draws a wan smile. "Plus disconnecting from corporate assholes will go a long way towards healing." Lisa frowns, but Jessica doesn't notice. "What I wouldn't give…"

"Wouldn't give for what?" Lisa asks, breaking the train of thought.

Jessica laughs, bright and sharp as broken glass. "After swimming with barracudas as long as I have, the opportunity to escape for a while, maybe forever, would be a miracle of the sea parting type. Borrowing money from yourself is an exceptionally small price to pay."

Lisa shakes her head. "I think I'm the only one on the planet who likes working with other people."

"Maybe you're an alien. Would answer a lot of questions," Jessica assures her and is rewarded with a laugh. "My sage advice is to forgive him, shame him into getting you something nice and reciprocate with moral support. Lots of it. He's going to need it."

Lisa walks around the desk and the two hug. A soft fragrance drifts from the girl, delivering summer, and all it promises, to the stuffy office. Tears threaten, but Jessica wills them away. *Battle-axes don't cry*, she reminds herself. Jessica pulls away and heads out the door. As she leaves, she calls over her shoulder, "Don't forget the specification."

Lisa doesn't answer. She is already bent over the document, appearing to focus this time.

Lisa examines the table setting. Crystal Pilsners and bone china are excessive for beer and pizza, but it's Alan's favorite meal and she wants to make amends. Anxiously she adjusts the settings one more time and waits for his arrival. Arrival... Today is a day of arrivals.

A spasm jerks through her face as Lisa remembers this morning. Crimson drops falling into the toilet, exploding into feathery blooms before fading into nothingness. It shouldn't have been a surprise; they'd been trying for at least six months and still—nothing. But every month hope rises from the ashes, only to crash and burn. She bites her lip while brushing at her eyes. One more crash and burn. So be it. There's always next month. The garage door rattles up, and she almost drops a plate. She slaps it on the table and steps back, trembling with excitement–and—fear?

The fear melts away when Lisa sees the dejected look on Alan's face. His shoulders stoop and he looks ten years older than last week. Without hesitation, she throws her arms around him and gives him a noisy kiss.

Bewildered, Alan returns both and then pulls back. "What's up, pretty lady?"

"Surprise," she cries and drags him over to the table.

Alan bursts out laughing. "What's the occasion?"

She grimaces. "My way of saying I'm sorry. Friends?"

"More than friends," he declares and kisses the top of her head. "So we're okay?"

"Definitely."

"Great, because today I found an oscilloscope on eBay that..."

Lisa stops him with a finger on his lips. "I will listen to every detail at length. But right now, I just want to eat pizza."

"No problem," Alan grins as they attack the feast.

6.

Knee-high by the Fourth of July. The rhyme tumbles in his head keeping time with the undulating green waves. A farmer had once told Alan that there wasn't any truth to that saying; that corn grew differently every year depending on conditions. How short or tall it was by the Fourth was no indication that the crop would be good or bad. Now the Farmer's Almanac. That is a different story... Alan smiles and tears his gaze away from the softly swaying corn. It's well over head-high, not just knee-high, but then, it is the end of August. End of August. *Huh.* He can't believe how time has flown by.

Leaving the office was easy. There was the packing and the insincere good-byes; even Bill had come by, looking for assurance that he wasn't the reason Alan was leaving. Alan had brushed him off, refusing to give an inch. That, along with the palpable jealousy, had felt good. Really good. Oh, and a going-away luncheon complete with strip-o-gram. Compliments of Steve. That had been embarrassing but also good. Exceptionally good. Now, Alan is glad it's all behind him and that he's doing so well. As well as expected.

Prior to the move, Alan had researched how to successfully work at home. He discovered some common themes. First: maintain a schedule and dress for the office. Every morning Alan gets up with Lisa, showers, shaves, and then dresses just as he had for Benton. A side benefit is that he has time to make them breakfast and they sit and talk before she leaves.

Establishing a work area isolated from the rest of the house is emphasized. One expert recommended soundproofing. Since Alan is the only one in the house most of the time, he decided not to set up a special office and made camp in the dining room instead. He winces remembering Lisa's blow-up.

Yeah, right. Like they really need a place for entertaining. The area is open, big enough to spread out and with proximity to the kitchen. Alan is making more progress than he has in years.

If there's a drawback, it's the pay schedule.

For his entire working life, Alan enjoyed the same two-week pay schedule that all the other lemmings received. Now it depends strictly on when he reaches his milestones. And he can't complain about the schedule; he'd set it himself. The first milestone is a week away. All he has to do is keep plowing and the rewards will come. *Plowing.* His mind drifts to the corn.

I'm Christopher Columbus, Alan thinks. *No, really Isabella, I'm not crazy, give me money for nothing. You won't be sorry. I'll come back. Promise."* The good queen probably looked just as grim as the assembly in the conference room. Should they gamble and dole out Benton's closely guarded funds? Or should they send him packing until he has something more concrete? Sweat trickles down Alan's back and the unfamiliar tie feels like a gag. *What is the temperature, anyway? A million degrees? Heart of the sun?* Steve is the only positive note, but he's strictly an observer. Alan scans the conference room as his mind wanders.

If he weren't so stressed, Alan would enjoy this room. A huge plate glass window, shaded by an ancient maple, gives a serene view of a pond. Ducks float peacefully on the water's surface.

"Alan. Earth to Alan." Neil, the project manager, is calling.

Alan refocuses. "Sorry, what's the question?"

"How do you feel about the past four weeks?"

"Fine, why?" Alan says. *What about the money?*

Steve interjects, "Too much time? Too little? Just right?"

"Oh, a Goldilocks' perspective..." Alan quips. The group laughs easily. He's the only nervous one. Of course, he has the most to lose.

"Sure," Neil says. "You don't have to adjust the schedule, but if you move in the timeline, you get your money sooner and the market gets a product quicker. Everybody wins."

"I noticed you didn't say what happens if it gets moved out," Alan comments.

"That's because it's obvious. Longer schedule: no money,

no product. Everyone loses," Phil remarks in an acrid tone. He glowered throughout the meeting, asking questions with no good answers. Alan is tired, so he decides to go for broke.

"Look, I've made this milestone, there's no reason to believe I won't make the next, and I still don't have any money. So what's it going to be, gentlemen? I've delivered, how about you?"

Neil laughs. "Same old Alan. Give no quarter; take no prisoners. God I miss having you around. Of course we'll deliver; you did a hell of a job." Relief floods through Alan and the temperature in the room plummets. Suddenly he feels cool.

Neil signs a form and hands it to Alan. "Here you go, spend it in good health. But seriously," he adds. "What about the schedule?"

Alan doesn't look at Phil, but he can sense the curmudgeon's eyes boring into the side of his head. "I'll think about it, but for now, let's leave it the way it is." Both Steve and Neil shrug, while Phil beams. Alan hates to disappoint his friends, but has no choice. *Damn it, they'll just have to deal with it. This hasn't been a cakewalk. Once I'm settled. Maybe. But not now.* The thoughts dissipate as Steve claps him on the back.

"Great job. You're definitely earning your pay."

"Thank god," Alan says, "I've got computers to pay off."

"I hear that. Listen, we still on for tomorrow night?"

"Of course, I'll even spring for steaks. Are you bringing Beth?"

Steve pauses. "I'd like to, but Lisa...."

"Don't worry about Lisa. She'll be so excited that I'm finally getting paid she'll put up with anyone." Noting Steve's cringe, Alan backtracks. "There's nothing wrong with Beth. She's just young, beautiful, smart, you know, all those things women hate. Unless of course they're completely self-assured. Like Lisa."

Steve laughs. "I'll be there; Beth in tow. You break the news to Lisa." He looks at his watch and says, "Uh-oh. Gotta run. Lunch meeting on a Friday."

"I was hoping we could catch lunch," Alan calls to the

quickly retreating back.

"Next time." Steve waves and is gone.

A weird desolation settles over Alan. Walking to payroll, he thinks of Lisa. She'd be up for lunch. The isolation dissipates and Alan hurries to get his first corp-to-corp pay check.

"The Potting Shed" is packed the way it is every Friday. The abundance of plants gives it a tropical air, further emphasized by the beach-type umbrellas over the patio tables. The menu, mostly overstuffed sandwiches and huge salads, makes the tiny restaurant popular year-round, but especially in the summer. To ensure getting a table, Lisa and Jessica took lunch early. As a result, at 11:30, the two are dubiously sizing up chef's salads.

"Just dig in," Jessica admonishes. "We are the predators, it is the prey. Don't let the fact that it's bigger than your head scare you."

"If you say so," Lisa says and attacks. A few minutes pass and then Jessica speaks up.

"How's the HAH project going?"

"HAH?" Lisa asks. "Not sure. I don't think I'm involved."

"Sure you are. You're co-leader. It's the Hubby At Home," Jess explains with a grin.

Lisa groans. "The name's horrible, but the project couldn't be better. Alan's eating better and he walks every day. His blood pressure is down and even his doctor can't believe the change. The best part is that he's actually fun to be around again."

Jessica arches her perfectly shaped eyebrows. "A man? Fun? Tell me another one."

Lisa ignores the sarcasm. "And, he makes me breakfast. I'm talking real quality time."

"Sounds perfect. I know people who'd kill for that kind of life. Me, for instance."

"Yep," Lisa concedes. "Pretty close to perfect." As soon as the words leave her mouth, Lisa regrets them. Before she can backtrack, Jessica pounces.

"Pretty close? All right, spill it. What fly has wandered into your ointment?"

For a second Lisa considers dodging the question, but she's terrible at subterfuge. Eventually Jessica will worm it out of her, and it would be nice to talk about it. "I haven't talked to anyone but Alan—and my doctor—about this and it's starting to eat me alive. He's sweet, but he just doesn't—can't—understand."

Alarm transforms Jessica's face. "What is it? Are you sick? Spit it out. Now."

Lisa smiles at the leap to worst case scenario. "I'm not dying." Jessica still looks doubtful. "Honest, it's more important than that. I—we're trying to have a baby." Lisa bursts out laughing at the look on Jessica's face. "It's not that unbelievable, is it?"

"No. Honey, no. I couldn't be happier for you. It's just that you've always been such a career girl. The anti-mom. This is the last thing I expected. You two'll make great parents."

"Maybe. If it happens," Lisa says, focusing on the huge pile of salad left on her plate.

"What do you mean, if?"

"We've been trying for over six months and nothing."

Jessica munches thoughtfully on a radish. When it's gone, she says, "I can't speak from experience, but that doesn't sound like a long time. What does your doctor say?"

"Same thing. She said that if nothing happens within two years or so, we can start looking deeper. The problem is that I want it now. Not two years from now. Look at how old I'll be," she says, disliking the whine in her voice.

"Right," Jessica agrees.

Lisa winces at her friend's dry tone.

"You'll be, what, thirty-seven? Oooooh, ancient…"

"Well, it feels ancient."

"Honey, when you get to my age, we can talk about ancient. Lots of women have babies in their forties these days. Even fifties, god forbid. Stop worrying."

"I'm scared. My career should have waited instead of children."

"Don't second-guess your decisions. Everything you've

done has made you the person you are," Jessica scolds. "Why do you want children anyway? Why now?"

Lisa sighs. "I can't explain it. I just woke up one day and decided it was time. My biological clock wasn't just ticking, the alarm was clanging."

"See, now that's my point. Before this, you weren't ready. It wouldn't have been right to bring a child into the world. Now you're ready. The time is right. Just be patient."

"But what about the extra expense? Isn't this a bad time to get pregnant?"

"Excuse me ladies, but is everything okay with your meal?" asks a hovering manager.

"What?" Lisa snaps.

"Your meal, is everything okay? You've hardly touched your salads."

"Everything's fine," Jessica interjects firmly. "Thank you. Go away." The man nods and moves to the next table.

Lisa chokes back a laugh. "Jess, he's just doing his job."

"I don't care about him or his job. I care about you. Now, where were we?"

"Isn't this a bad time…" Lisa repeats and takes a bite of her neglected salad.

"That's another thing I know for sure. There's no good time to have a baby. Just go for it and everything'll be fine." And she attacks her lunch as well.

7.

The last milestone is a sweet distant dream. Now Alan has to concentrate on the next one and this phase isn't going as smoothly as the first. Alan takes a few precious moments to think about the conversation he'd had with Steve that Saturday night. *What is Steve thinking?*

Steve and Beth came over as promised and Lisa had been on her best behavior, also as promised. Soon after he arrived, Steve maneuvered Alan into a private conversation.

"Tell me the truth, Alan, is the schedule for real?"

Alan frowned. "Whatta you mean?"

Steve looked out across the perfectly manicured lawn, still green and fresh in spite of the moratorium, and watched the fireflies for a few seconds. "Don't get me wrong. You've done everything you said you would. And more. Neil knows it; I know it. It's just that this product is hot. I suspect our competitor has something similar on the back burner. If they beat us to market, we're dead."

"I can appreciate that, but this is the schedule we agreed to. I'm doing the best I can."

"That's all I wanted to hear. I know you'll give it your best. I'd never question that. Just keep in mind that if you can tighten it up, you'll be a hero." Steve paused for emphasis. "Bring it in enough—there might even be a bonus."

Before Alan could answer, Lisa broke in, eyes rolling frantically at her husband. She'd been alone with Beth too long. Averting a potential homicide was more important than Steve's comment; Alan ran to her aid. Since then he'd thought about that conversation a lot.

Alan sighs. He's doing his best. He is. It's just that the schematic laid out on the monitor had a malignant quality. He'd designed it. He should understand it. But he doesn't. It teases and dances just out of reach, refusing to cooperate. The analysis program is useless; the data it spews out is nonsense. Wearily he rubs his eyes, hearing as well as feeling, the blood pulsing through his head. He pauses, listening more carefully to the sound. It isn't in his head; it's—where? Alan stands, dislodging Gandalf from his lap in the process, and goes to the window. The sight both excites and dismays him.

Last week, the next door lot had 'Sold' plastered across its sign. Today, heavy machinery is excavating. That's the pounding. While Lisa will be happy, Alan wishes they'd picked another start time. Like when he doesn't have to concentrate.

He returns to the dining room and the schematic. Minutes tortuously tick by, revealing nothing new except for sounds from the construction site. Alan now hears kids. He can't blame them. It's summer and he'd be out there with them if he wasn't chained to this job.

In frustration, Alan pushes back from the table and wanders into the kitchen. A can of Mountain Dew and a Zinger make him feel better for about thirty seconds. He grabs another cake and then puts it back. He's only eating because his mouth is bored. Better find something else to do. Looking around, he sees the basement door. *Why not? Just for a little while. A virtual cigarette break if you will.* Quickly, he moves to the door and is through and going down the stairs before his conscience can stop him.

Alan jumps at the slamming kitchen door. He lays down the model plane and looks at his watch. *It can't possibly be that late.* He looks twice just to make sure. *Yep. Six o'clock. Damn. Busted.* He frantically sorts through his options. *The truth? Only as a last resort. Nonchalance. That's it. No big deal.* Mind made up, Alan heads up the stairs.

"Hey pretty lady," he calls out.

"Where are you?" Lisa asks.

"Oh, I got done early and gave myself a break. How was your day?"

Lisa refuses to bite. "Fine. What do you mean, early?"

"Why is everyone harping about the schedule?" Alan demands, his complexion a bright color that hadn't been seen in months. "What's wrong with meeting the schedule? That's what I signed up for. I'm only human, for God's sake."

"And that's fine. I only asked because you said you got done early. That's all."

Alan calms down some, but still has a way to go. "Well, we know what assume means."

"I said I was sorry. So what were you doing?"

"Working on my new plane." There's that damn tight-lipped expression. Alan knows he has to come clean. Taking a deep breath, he admits, "Look, I'm stuck. A short break to clear my head seemed like a good idea and the next thing I knew the day was gone. I'll make up the time, I promise." He tries a smile. "I'll just make myself work overtime. But no extra pay," he admonishes solemnly, shaking a finger for emphasis.

Lisa gives a tight shrug, still frowning. "I guess a short break isn't the end of the world."

"Just think of it as a virtual cigarette break."

"Uh-huh. Honestly, Alan, this is rationalization."

Rage nibbles at his brain, but this isn't the time. Not when he's guilty. Undeniably guilty. "Maybe, but construction noise was getting to me." That does it. She beams.

"It's inconvenient, but just think. Neighbors... A real community..."

The alarm clock is exceptionally irritating. In a fit of remorse, Alan had decided to go back to work after dinner. Unfortunately, spaghetti and Chianti had won out over good intentions, and he was just too tired. Alan opted for FreeCell instead of schematics. Disapproval oozed from Lisa in an acrid cloud, but Alan ignored her. *I'd rather spend time thinking through the problem instead of rushing in when I'm tired and then have to redo it. Too tired to explain I'm backbraining the problem, not procrastinating.*

"More rationalization, Alan? Hmmm?" she'll say. *And then she'll get that look. I'd rather she stalked around glaring than get the look.*

Long after she'd gone to bed, Alan had stayed up matching wits with the computer. And now here he is, eyes gritty, body aching. Four hours of sleep doesn't hack it.

"Do you want the shower first?" Lisa asks, eyes still closed.

"You go ahead. I'm sleeping in today." Funny how censure can be felt even when delivered in silence. Of course, she's rigid and her breathing has practically stopped. It doesn't take a psychic to guess what she's thinking.

"What do you mean, sleeping in?" She's up on one elbow, no longer drowsy.

"I was up late. I won't be worth much without a little more sleep. I'll make it up."

Teeth clenched, she forces out, "Like last night?"

"No, last night I was thinking through the design. Today and tonight," he stresses 'tonight', "I'll put those ideas into place." He pauses but she says nothing. "Haven't you ever heard 'Work smart, not hard'? Well, this is working smart. Next, I'll work hard."

Lisa studies him for a second then rolls out of bed. "I guess this means breakfast is out?"

"Yeah. Sorry. I'll make that up, too."

"No worries. I survived before, I'll survive again."

The shower starts and that's the last thing Alan hears until afternoon.

By the time Alan showers, eats and sits before the computer, the construction crew is in full swing. Its din fills the house. Dave's makeshift drumming seems trivial in comparison. Around three, Alan gives up and escapes to the basement. This time, he keeps a close eye on the clock and is in front of the computer before Lisa gets home. She doesn't comment, but he can tell she's trying to assess his progress. Dinner is strained, but they suffer through and eventually ease into a normal evening. Neither brings up the stalled project.

The rest of the week follows the same pattern. Alan stays up later and later, subsequently sleeping in longer. Concentration in the dining room is a lost cause. Even with all the windows closed and the air conditioner on, the noise from the construction site echoes through the house. Alan reasons that it won't last long and then he can resume working, energized from taking a short break.

These thoughts flow dreamily as he works on his plane in the basement's quiet coolness. Soon, it will be in the air. He looks out the window and into the sunshine. Puffy white clouds drift in the blue infinity. His plane swoops in and out, a silver bird free in the heavens.

He frowns. "How will I explain finishing it? She's not going to buy the old virtual cigarette break." He's the one who'd gone on about how much time and effort these things take. *Damn.* With a shrug, he bends over the plane and is soon lost in the intricacies of the motor.

As he works, Alan realizes he's missing an assembly. He tries to remember where he'd put it. "I know I bought one," he announces. Nothing disturbs the stillness. Not even Gandalf. Even though he constantly wanders through the dining room, the big tom never ventures into the basement. Drumming his fingers on the bench, Alan retraces the day he bought the piece.

Suddenly, he snaps his fingers and spins around, heading for the middle cabinet in a group of three. Throwing open doors, he scans the disorganized shelves and finds the missing part. Halfway to the bench, he stops, his senses focused on an almost indiscernible sound.

At first he can't tell where it's coming from because it disappears as soon as he stops. He waits, ears straining. Then it comes again, a faint, rustling sound, like leaves whispering across concrete. He whirls in the direction of the noise and it's gone. It seems as tuned to him as he is to it. Maybe more. He sees a stack of boxes. *Of course; varmints hide in boxes. Lisa said she'd put this stuff away. I'm not the only one who procrastinates...* Alan moves towards the stack and grabs the closest carton.

Soon, the boxes are away from the wall. The floor is clean, completely free of the expected droppings. "Okay," he declares, flinching at the echo, "You must be in the boxes."

Outwardly, the cartons look inviolate. No gnawed holes, no loose flaps inviting visitors. He remembers taping them shut for that reason. Shrugging, Alan opens each one and inspects the contents. Nothing.

"Imagination," he says to himself. "Maybe something outside that just sounded like it was in here." Dissatisfied, but not sure what else to do, he starts searching drawers for strapping tape. The voice that snaps in his ear almost stops his heart.

"What are you doing?" Lisa demands.

Alan glances at his watch. Four o'clock. "What are you doing home so early?"

"It doesn't matter. What I want to know is, what the hell are you doing?"

"Looking for tape," Alan snaps back. "I need to seal the boxes."

Lisa looks over the jumble. "I can see that. Did you go on your scavenger hunt before or after you finished that?" she asks, pointing to the plane.

"Ah—well—uh—it's not finished." Trapped, he tries a stronger tone. "It wasn't a scavenger hunt. I was looking for something in particular," he says, gesturing to the assembly on the bench. Too late, he realizes it only nails the coffin shut. Lisa's eyebrows arch and Alan hurries on. "Forget that. I heard something in the boxes."

"Like what?"

"A scrabbling noise. Like mice."

Lisa frowns. "It's a brand new house. How can we have mice?"

"Age doesn't matter. They can get in any place."

"Did you find droppings?"

"No, but I'm sure I heard something."

His wife waves her hand in dismissal. "It's probably something outside or the air conditioner kicking on." A flush creeps up Alan's neck. Lisa continues. "However, that doesn't explain why you're down here at all. And playing with your toys when you should be working."

Alan winces. "They're not t—" he starts but is cut off by anger he's never seen in Lisa.

Her voice icy and sharp, she says, "I don't care what you call them. They're distractions. What real work did you do today?"

"Better question. Why are you home? Are you checking up on me?" he snaps back. "I don't have to give you a report on my every move."

"When you act like this you do. When was the last time you actually did anything?"

Alan stares at his workbench, his plane huddled in the middle of scattered debris. The shit's deep enough. Up to his chin. Head lowered, he mumbles, "Don't know."

"What was that?"

Flinching, he makes eye contact. "I said, I don't know."

Lisa shakes her head, lips pinched so tight they're white around the edges. She takes a deep breath. "Okay," she says with a loud exhalation. "You're stuck. What do you normally do when you get stuck?"

"Talk to somebody."

"Okay, so why don't you call somebody?"

"Everyone will think I can't handle this on my own."

"Right now, I'd agree."

The words are a slap. Harsh and stinging. "That's not fair." It comes out as a whine.

"No? From where I sit, as soon as you lost supervision, you lost discipline. Maybe you can't handle working alone."

Anger surges, but inward. He takes a deep breath and agrees. "Maybe I can't."

Dismay creeps in and slowly pushes the fury out of Lisa's eyes. She holds up her hands in a gesture of helplessness. "So what do we do? Sell the stuff? Admit you made a mistake?"

"No. I can do it; I just have to get back on track."

"How?"

"Look, you were right about the dining room. Concentration is impossible. I need a secluded work area, a real office."

"Where?"

"Down here," Alan says, throwing his arms out to

encompass the open area. "I feel more relaxed and there aren't any distractions. I should've done this from the beginning."

Lisa frowns. "I thought you said it'd take too much money. Too much time. Won't you have to stop work until it's ready?"

"No, I can work at my bench. I'll rig something for the Internet connection and run extension cords for the outlets. The remodeling I'll do at night and on the weekends. Hell, I figure I'll draft Steve. His ass is on the line, too."

A smile flickers across Lisa's lips. "And mine. We sink or swim together."

Alan grins. "I'll count on your ass any day, pretty lady."

"Don't try to sweet talk your way out of this. I'm still mad and you haven't convinced me you can do this. We've got too much riding on it to have it screwed up."

Alan consciously relaxes his clenched jaw before answering. "You're right," he forces out. "Tell you what. I'll make you a deal. How does a daily status report sound?"

"That's not necessary," Lisa protests, but the words are empty. It's obvious that she likes the idea.

"It'll be good for me," Alan assures her. "A way to track my progress. I'll start tomorrow."

"All right, it's a deal," she says and sticks out her hand.

Alan pumps it vigorously and then pulls her to him, enveloping her small frame in a bear hug. She resists for just a moment, a moment so short he wonders if he imagined it, then returns the embrace. He kisses the top of her head.

"Still love me?" he asks.

"Of course." The answer is muffled. "Just worried."

"Understandable... Tell you what, let's start right now. Help me move my stuff down so I can get a full day in tomorrow."

"Great idea," she says moving towards the stairs. "We can call for pizza."

8.

Steve stands in the middle of the basement, beer in hand, and tries to visualize the layout. "I understand a bathroom, but why a kitchen?"

Alan stops in the middle of his animated description. "Cuts down on distractions. This way, I can make a quick snack then hit it again with minimal time loss."

His friend drinks from the dew-speckled bottle. "Quoting from one of your handbooks?"

"Yep."

Steve shakes his head, "I dunno. It's a good idea to break away once in a while."

"Yeah, but if I'm on a roll, I don't want to stop and leave just because I'm hungry. Given my recent performance, the more I'm confined to one room the better off I'm going to be."

Steve reluctantly agrees. He hadn't told Alan how worried he'd been when Lisa told him what happened. Nobody, not even his best friends, know how much is riding on this venture. *If a kitchen keeps him focused, fine. Hell, I'll hire a chef if I have to.*

Alan adds, "Plus it adds value to the house. Now there's a mother-in-law suite."

Steve looks around. "Why aren't you closer to the stairs?"

"It's more isolated this way. The psychological disconnect of walking across an open area to an 'office' will more strongly implant the difference between 'home' and 'office'."

"Another book? I hope?" Steve asks with a smile.

"Yep. The second reason—me, no book—is the window. The cornfield's peaceful."

Steve studies the pastoral view and agrees, sipping his beer in silence.

Stomachs pleasantly full, the foursome sit on the deck and watched the sun go down on another perfect summer day.

Surprisingly, August has been mild and pleasant, unlike the sweltering July. Fragrant smoke from citronella torches drifts lazily on the soft breeze, lending a surrealistic air to the evening. Steve is the first to break the silence.

"Alan, when are you starting on the office?"

"I'm drawing up a floor plan. Once that's finished I can get going."

"Do you need help?"

"All I can get," Alan remarks quickly.

Steve laughs at his friend's eagerness. "I guess I walked into that one. Count me in. When do we start?"

"Next weekend if that's okay."

"I don't see a problem with that," Steve says and takes a drink of beer.

Beth never says much around Lisa, but this draws her out. "What do you mean next weekend?" she blurts. "We're going to Marcie's. It's been planned for months."

Steve shrugs. "There's something planned every weekend. Marcie and the gang are just going to have to get along without us." He pauses. "Of course, you can go. Just tell'em something came up."

Beth flushes, the color aping her scarlet hair. "I'm not going alone," she sulks.

"Suit yourself," Steve says. He shakes his head in exasperation as he studies the two women. One pouting—one smirking.

Then, the younger one brightens. "I've got an idea," Beth chirps. "I'll come help."

Lisa's smirk turns to horror. "Thanks for the offer, but there won't be much for you to do. And I'll feel terrible if you miss your party," she adds, her lame attempt at concern falling flat.

Steve looks at Beth, but it's Alan that steps in.

"Don't be ridiculous," Alan interjects. "There's plenty to do. You sure you don't mind?" The last statement is directed at Beth.

"Of course not," Beth purrs.

Steve grins, too much of a coward to meet Lisa's eyes.

"What's on the agenda, Alan?"

"Everything except for the rough in on the plumbing and the gas line for the stove. I'll contract those out."

Steve winces. "Ouch. What's this going to cost?"

Alan cuts a quick look at Lisa and then back to Steve. "It's not pretty. Another ten grand." Steve gives a low whistle. "And that's being optimistic," Alan adds.

"Where will you get the money?" Beth asks. Steve wishes he'd explained the situation better to his hapless date. Now he has to sit and watch as Lisa skewers her with glaring eyes.

"We'll borrow against my 401K," Lisa replies flatly.

"Your retirement fund?" Beth twists the dagger, oblivious to the pain she causes.

"Yes."

The young redhead shrugs. "Then why do it?"

"We're in too deep," Alan explains. "We have to."

Beth opens her mouth but Steve can't let her go on. "I'm tired of just sitting; let's go check out the new houses."

"Sure," Alan agrees, relieved to be out of the hot seat. "Maybe we can hotwire a bulldozer or something."

"Can you do that?" Beth exclaims.

Lisa rolls her eyes at Steve who laughs and gives Beth a quick squeeze. "Won't know 'til we try," he says as they head toward the construction site.

Monday morning and Alan is once again standing in the basement explaining the office layout. This time it's to Big Bob McClanahan and his brother, Little Bill, the twins that own and operate Big Bob's Plumbing.

"Yep. We can fix you right up," Big Bob heartily assures him.

"Right up," Little Bill agrees.

Alan had always thought of himself as a big man, but the twins dwarf him, each roughly the size of a semi-truck. The names seem curious since they are completely identical, but Bob explained. "See, I was born first and weighed 5 lbs. Bill here," he gestured at his sibling with a meaty paw, "came next at a measly 4 1/2 lbs. We been making up for lost time ever since, but Bill's always lagged b'hind."

"Lagged b'hind," Bill nodded in amiable agreement.

Now, they stand side by side, blocking out the sun and disrupting the tides, giving Alan an estimate. "What's the damage?" he asks.

Again, the hearty laugh with accompanying echo. "The only damage is when we bust a hole in your floor," Bob says, Bill choking on his older brother's wit.

"Right. Got it. Very funny. What's it going to cost?" Alan snaps.

Big Bob frowns but becomes all business. "You know, you'd live longer if you'd lighten up a bit. Let's see. Rough in for the toilet, water lines, gas for the stove...." As he talks, he marks each item down on a grubby envelope with a chewed pencil stub. He pauses. "Do you want all the plumbing done or just the rough in?"

"Are you handling all the permits and code stuff?

"Yep. Part and parcel," Big Bob nods.

"Part and parcel," Little Bill repeats.

"I guess so, then."

"It comes to just over five, but since you're such a nice guy we'll call it five grand even."

Alan feels his heart sink. "When can you start?"

An answering grin. "How 'bout Tuesday?"

"Works for me," Alan says, letting the two mount the stairs first. He stays well back in case of a collapse. In spite of the creaking, the brothers make it up without incident and Alan returns to his computer. Outside, bulldozers rattle along unnoticed.

The plumber brothers are true to their word and appear Tuesday morning, jackhammer ready to go. Alan groans, realizing the construction has moved inside. He follows the pair to the basement and asks, "How long will it take to do the floor?"

"Well, ripping the floor up is the easy part," Big Bob

observes.

"Yeah," Little Bill adds. "Putting it back's the tough part." The line feels like a rehearsed joke; one used often and still receiving the laughs it deserves, at least from the brothers. Their laughter is so contagious that Alan smiles in spite of himself.

"Okay," he breaks in, "How long will that take?"

Big Bob wipes his eyes with the back of his fist and manages to choke out, "Seriously—mmm—coupla days we should have the concrete setting up."

"Setting up" Bill agrees. Alan leaves them to their work and returns to his.

The jackhammer isn't as much of a distraction as Alan feared it would be, thanks to earplugs. Breaking for lunch, he brings his sandwich down to the basement along with sodas for the jumbo brothers. The food reminds them that they are in danger of losing some of their girth, so they break as well. As Alan bites into his puny sandwich he notices that the McClanahan lunches are as impressive as the brothers.

Talking around a mouthful, Alan asks, "Have you guys noticed any noises down here?"

The brothers look at each other, shrug and then look back at Alan. "What kind of noises?"

"I don't know, rustlings, scrapings, anything unusual."

"You mean like rats?" Bob asks.

"Maybe mice. I wouldn't expect rats."

Bob shakes his head. "You don't want rats," he declares solemnly.

"Don't want rats," Bill agrees.

"Okay, okay, no rats," Alan says, "But anything else?"

"Nah," the older brother remarks, forehead screwed up in concentration, "of course with all the noise we been making, probably wouldna heard anything, anyway. Maybe we ran 'em off." He chews for a while then adds "But I know a guy, best rat guy in the area, that can get rid of any varmint guar—one— teed."

Bill chimes in. "Earl?"

"Yep."

"Guar—one—teed," Bill agrees heartily, eyes shining at the mention of he who is obviously a god among exterminators.

"Thanks, but no thanks. It's not that big a deal."

Big Bob shrugs. Slight delay. Little Bill shrugs.

"Suit yourself," Bob says, "but you really don't want rats."

Surprisingly, Alan is sorry to see the brothers go. They'd been a welcome change from the isolation. On his way out, Big Bob insists on giving Alan a phone number; Earl - Exterminator Extraordinaire. Not wanting to argue, Alan thanks him and tucks the slip of paper away. After all the money he'd just laid out, he isn't about to pay somebody to get rid of a few mice.

9.

The next Saturday, Steve shows up to help with the remodeling. Lisa meets him at the door with a hug and a kiss.

"What gives?" Steve asks, returning the embrace, and then holding her at arm's length.

"I'm just happy to see you," Lisa replies, "So—umm—did Beth decide to bug out?" The question is innocent enough, but too sugary-sweet for Lisa.

Imitating her sweet tone, he replies, "No, she's just running late." Steve has to hide a laugh as her face drops. Two points for Beth. It would have been three, but Lisa recovers quickly, hustling Steve into the basement where Alan is already at work putting up 2x6 framing.

"Relax, the Calvary's here," Steve announces.

Rolling his eyes as he stops hammering, Alan says, "It's about time, where's Beth?"

"If I didn't know better, I'd say you're more excited about Beth coming over than me."

"And that's a surprise?"

"No, a relief," Steve admits, ignoring the muscle twitching in Lisa's cheek. "I'm worried enough without adding questions about your sexual preferences to the mix."

Alan didn't laugh with Steve. "What do you mean, worried?"

"Lighten up buddy, it's just a joke."

Alan hesitates, then says, "It's okay. I've worried a lot of people. That's why the little slave driver over there is making me turn in status reports."

"You volunteered," Lisa protests but her smile gives her away.

"I think it's a great idea," Steve interjects. "Can you send copies to me and Neil? We can use them to supplement the design reviews."

Alan begins hammering. "Sure. Now, are you going to help

or stand there jabbering?"

"Call me when you're ready for drywall," Lisa says and heads up the stairs.

Steve selects a board.   "Why are you using 2 x 6's? Wouldn't 2 x 4's be cheaper?"

"Uh-huh, but I want to insulate the walls. I can't do that with 2 x 4's."

"Insulate?"

"Soundproofing, actually."

"Damn. The way you're building this thing, it can double as a bomb shelter. Nuclear war, tornadoes, you name it, this room'll still be standing." Steve pauses and then adds, "Of course, you'll be oblivious to anything beyond your perimeter."

Alan grins. "That's the whole idea. I'll just keep working."

Steve grins back and holds up a board for Alan to nail into place. The two work quickly and walls take shape. Eventually, Steve hears footsteps. He and Alan look up to see Lisa followed closely by Beth.

Bib shorts and a painter's cap that hide her shining mass of curls make Beth look like a poster girl for Sherwin-Williams. Lisa, wearing stained gray sweats and a torn tee shirt, isn't smiling.

"Hey, lady, glad you could make it," Steve says, greeting Beth with a peck on the cheek.

"Oh, I wouldn't miss this for the world," Beth assures him and grins at Lisa. Lisa shrugs and inspects the framing progress.

"Lisa, what can Beth do?" Alan asks, giving the girl a quick hug.

Without looking away from the 2x6's, Lisa says, "Nothing that won't ruin her outfit."

"Don't worry about me," Beth chirps, "this ol' rag has been around forever."

"All right. This desk needs stripping," Lisa says, gesturing to a large desk painted a hideous shade of yellow. "Garage sale treasure. Alan thinks it can be salvaged."

Lisa's on the brink of triumph, but Steve steps in before Beth can cave.   With his encouragement, his girlfriend's quickly immersed in restoring the ugly desk. Lisa goes upstairs after Beth begins, but periodically returns to checks up on the work. The fourth trip down, she stops at the desk, which is showing bare wood.

Beth looks up and asks, "What do you think?" Some curls have come loose from her cap and are plastered against her forehead. She looks earnest and vulnerable—human.

Lisa relents. "You're doing great. You know," she says, running her hand over the smooth grain. "I think that's oak.

Alan and Steve look at the desk. "Wow," Alan says. "I only paid forty bucks for that."

"At least something's on budget," Lisa adds.

Steve glances at Alan but he doesn't look up from the desk. Steve and Beth join him in his examination, while Lisa stands back, arms crossed. As the three drift back to work, Lisa disappears back upstairs.

It's late when they quit. The room is defined, but just barely. Starved and worn-out, the group digs into Lisa's only claim to culinary success, spaghetti. Steve notices that this is the first time he'd ever seen Beth eat without bringing up her latest diet. He watches the two women talk, afraid to say anything that might jinx this strange new camaraderie. They break up around ten, promising an early start the next morning. Steve isn't sure about his friends, but once at home, he goes right to bed, sliding into dreamless sleep without needing his usual double Jack on the rocks.

The next day Beth continues her work on the desk, but this time with Lisa's help. At first, Steve is tense, but there doesn't seem to be any underlying motives. Stopping only for a quick lunch, the four work through the day and quit around eight.

"Anyone for a beer?" Alan ask.

Steve declines, his arm resting companionably around Beth's shoulders. "Thanks, guy, but we'd better be heading home," Steve says, reluctantly. A beer does sound good.

"Okay. See you next weekend?" Alan asks, not even trying

to hide his desperation.

"You bet. How about you, kid?" Steve directs this question towards the girl tucked under his arm.

Beth snuggles up closer and nods.

Steve smiles. "Count us in." With a wave at Alan and Lisa, he guides her towards the red Corvette and squeezes her shoulders. "Thanks," he murmurs, "You're a big help."

"It wasn't any trouble at all," Beth assures him and laughs. "At first I did it just to piss Lisa off, but I wound up enjoying myself."

"Good." He opens her door and then gets in the driver's seat. "I'm kind of sorry the weekend's over," he says.

"It doesn't have to be," Beth suggests.

Pretending not to understand, Steve asks, "What'd you have in mind?" The girl leans over and puts both hands behind his neck pulling him close as she curves her body into his. Soft, full lips meet his, her tongue probing gently. When he finally pulls away, he blinks to clear his head.

She laughs softly. "Maybe we can extend the weekend. At my place," she breathes, one hand trailing down his chest. Steve can feel the urgency mounting.

"Sounds like an offer I can't refuse," he replies in a raspy voice. Without any more discussion, the engine roars to life and the car disappears into the night.

Alan and Lisa stand on the front porch and watch the two get into the car. When the couple leans into their kiss, Alan walks with Lisa into the house, one arm curved around her waist. "Steve really seems to like her," he says.

"Uh-huh..."

"What's wrong? I thought you two were getting along."

"Yeah…"

"Then what?" Alan snaps, too tired for games.

"It's just that he seems so serious and he doesn't even know her," Lisa bursts out.

"What are you talking about? I know people who've gotten married quicker than that."

"I know, I know. I just worry about him."

Alan sighs. "Steve's a big boy. He has a right to make his own decisions and—his own mistakes."

"You're right," Lisa admits and walks to the refrigerator, taking out a beer.

After taking the bottle, Alan gives her a kiss on the cheek. "I'm going to watch television. Join me?" he says.

"In a minute. I want to clean up first."

"Okay," he calls out, moving towards the family room. Lisa sees a gray shadow dart in behind him.

Lisa stumbles up the stairs and then turns the water up as hot as she can stand it. But although the scalding stream colors her skin lobster red, it doesn't even dent the gray cocoon that embraces her. *I should join Alan, but...* The unfinished thought swirls round and round as she puts on her flannel gown and slides into bed. Her feather pillow is soaked with tears by the time she finally drifts off to sleep.

For the first time in over a month Alan feels confident. Every day is split into contract work and the office. They made great progress over the weekend and he's sure they will again, but the thought of being done and in his own space is becoming an obsession.

With Lisa's assistance, Alan finishes the framing late Tuesday night. Wednesday is wiring. He needs lots of outlets, good lighting and dedicated data lines in addition to the phone. By Friday, it's done and covered with insulation, ready for drywall.

Saturday morning, as promised, Steve shows with Beth in tow. The layout is simple and, as a result, the drywall goes up quickly. The men hang the sheets by noon and Beth takes a break from the desk, helping Lisa with the spackling. Watching the two women work together, laughing and talking, it's hard to believe that a month ago they were at each other's throats.

While Lisa and Beth are trowel-ling, Alan and Steve install the kitchenette. The foursome work diligently until late Saturday night and pick up Sunday morning. By late evening, the kitchen is in and most of the drywall is spackled and sanded. Alan thinks they can get everything done in another two weeks.

Alan's prediction is wrong. A week is all it takes. That Saturday night, the tired couples stand inside the office, amazed at their accomplishment. The workspace is arranged with an eye to aesthetics as well as efficiency. The kitchenette hugs two thirds of the back wall in a long, gallery-like arrangement and even includes a small dishwasher. The bathroom is angled at the end of the wall.

The rest of the room comprises the office with the refinished desk facing the window. Behind it, in the middle of the room, are a couch and a coffee table. A flat panel television covers the largest wall.

"I'm impressed," Lisa says, "but it still seems like overkill."

"Why?" Alan asks.

"This is more like an efficiency apartment than an office. Why does it have to be so elaborate when you can just go up the stairs?"

Alan is sick of this question. It wouldn't be so bad if anybody ever listened to his answer, but... "Staying focused is critical." He grits his teeth as Lisa starts in. Again.

"Look, I like it, you've done a great job," she says. "But this —it could be a bomb shelter."

"That's what I said," Steve adds, grinning.

"Even Steve agrees," Lisa says, her voice twisting into a whine. "I wish you'd get rid of those silly books. They're at the heart of this nonsense."

"Now hold on," Alan says, trying to keep his voice down but failing. "Those 'silly' books are written by experts. They know what they're talking about."

"Really? Well, I'd like to talk to one of them and see if they've built their own fortress of solitude. Look at this door. Why do you need a deadbolt?" To punctuate, she shoves the door and slams the deadbolt home. It connects with a finality that makes the other three jump. For a second, there's silence except for the clang reverberating against the walls. Then Lisa whirls around. "Forget your friggin' experts, I want to talk to the wives. They're the ones that have to deal with this madness."

Beth shivers. "It is kind of creepy with the door shut. I never knew any place could sound so quiet." Steve puts his arm around her and she leans into him.

Alan sighs and shakes his head. "Look, guys, this is a party. Maybe I did go a little overboard, but it's done. Sweetheart," he says, directing his comment to Lisa. "Give it a couple of weeks. If it still freaks you out, the deadbolt's history. Okay?"

"Well..." Lisa says.

Steve speaks up. "Turn-about's fair play, isn't it?"

"I guess so, but..."

Alan feels his jaw clench and wills it to relax. "What?" he forces out.

"Isn't it enough that I promise not to disturb you?"

"I can't count on that. Look, just treat it as if I'm at the office away from the phone. That doesn't bother you, does it?"

"No..."

"All right then. You'll get used to it. I promise," he says and kisses the top of her head. Lisa continues to glare at the door, but doesn't say anything.

Beth, however, does. "What happens if you have an accident or something? It could be days before anyone realizes something's wrong."

Coming from Beth, the concern isn't as—nagging. More endearing. "Don't worry about it," Alan says with a smile. "There's my cell phone and a landline. The window. And, most important, I'd like to think someone will miss me." With this, he hugs Lisa. She hesitates, then smiles and hugs him back.

Steve, voice booming, orders, "Quit the mushy stuff and break out the champagne."

"Amen," Alan agrees, walking to the refrigerator. The mood elevates considerably when the cork pops.

Sunday dawns clear and beautiful. Alan and Lisa are up early, eager to put the finishing touches on the office. Since the equipment is already in the basement, it's a simple job to transfer everything to the new space. There's a moment of alarm when the computer doesn't come on, but this passes when Alan realizes the breaker isn't reset on the surge protector.

Lisa focuses on the kitchen. In addition to flatware and dishes, she puts away the groceries: ravioli, stew, soups and chow mien. All of it is one-pot, warm in the microwave type food. She even remembered cookies.

"I'd forgotten the kitchen stuff. That would've sucked," Alan says, watching Lisa line up cans on the shelf. Lisa stops and turns around.

"Alan, have you heard any more noises?"

"No." His brow furrows in concentration. "No, not since I started working down here."

"Maybe you chased them away—oh—I'm missing a bag. I'll go get it. Be right back." She leaves the office and hurries up the stairs, taking the steps two at a time.

Lisa stands in the middle of the bedroom trying to remember what she did with the errant groceries. Wanting to surprise Alan, she'd hidden them in her closet, but she thought she had them all. Checking one more time, she notices a dress had fallen off the hanger and is draped over the missing bag. Triumphantly, she snags it and heads towards the basement.

Passing through the kitchen, she almost trips over Gandalf, who's decided he needs attention. The gray cat rubs against her legs, his purr rumbling louder than a lawn mower. Hooking the bag over one arm, she scoops him up and cradles him against her chest. He closes his eyes and purrs louder, rubbing his cheek against hers. Once he's situated, Lisa heads for the basement.

Halfway down the stairs, Lisa feels Gandalf tense. His purr disappears abruptly as his eyes snap open. He looks around, startled at such odd surroundings. Lisa strokes his fur while murmuring. Just before she reaches floor level, an angry growl rumbles in his chest. His eyes glow with a savage green light and Lisa starts to set him down, but not fast enough. Gandalf is gone and in his place is a hissing maelstrom that leaps out of her arms, leaving scarlet trails behind. Blood wells up and drips onto the concrete floor. Without hesitation, the cat shoots up the stairs and disappears into the kitchen.

Crossing the expanse from the stairs to the office, Lisa tries unsuccessfully to staunch the blood. The trip takes forever, her path marked by scarlet breadcrumbs, but finally she pushes open the steel door and shoves the bag at Alan. "I'm wounded," she announces, moving towards the sink.

"What happened?"

"I have no idea. I was bringing Gandalf down and he went nuts. Don't worry, the scratches look a lot worse than they really are."

"You sure?"

"Yeah, they sting a bit, but I'll be fine." She runs the water a little longer, and then applies fresh paper towels to the oozing wounds. "Didn't you hear the commotion? You'd have thought I was killing him by the way he was carrying on."

"No," he admits, "The soundproofing did its job. I didn't hear a thing."

"Huh. By the way, I now know firsthand where the word caterwauling came from…" She adds, "I'd better go upstairs and put some salve on these. I don't want them to get infected. Which reminds me, we need to stock your medicine cabinet. I'll go to the store tomorrow," she says as she leaves the room.

In the living room, she hears a low growl and looks under the couch. All the way at the back, she can make out two glowing eyes. Lisa leaves him alone, but she's worried. *Has he ever been in the basement? Hmmm… 'Course, does it matter? Oh damn…* The last thought is in response to the blood dripping from her arm onto the carpet. The tom's curious behavior is forgotten as she runs for the bathroom.

By the time Steve and Beth show up, everything is finished. The only thing left to do is relax. Once situated on the deck, Beth notices the scratches. "Wow, what'd you tangle with?"

"Our cat freaked when I tried to take him down to the basement. I was hoping he'd catch Alan's mystery mice."

"Maybe the mice are bigger than you think," Steve offers.

Unlike Beth's normal breathless speech, the girl muses,

"There might be more truth to that than you realize."

"What do you mean?" asks Alan.

"Animals are more sensitive than we are. Maybe there's something more than mice down there," Beth explains. "The house is new, right? It hasn't had time to get a history. A bad history, right?" Lisa shivers even though the sun is bright and hot for a fall day.

Alan notices and rubs her arms. "You cold?"

"Just a momentary chill. I'm okay." Turning to Beth, she says, "Now that you mention it, something weird happened while the house was being built."

"It wasn't weird," Alan interjects. "It was just sad."

"What?" Beth and Steve ask in unison, each leaning forward in their chairs.

"The foreman had a heart attack and died in the basement," Lisa said.

"See," Alan says. "Nothing unusual or weird. Just sad."

"But he was only forty-two with no history of heart problems or being sick at all." Lisa protests. "He went down to check out a water leak and his crew found him lying in the back of the basement. At first the guys thought he was sleeping, he looked that peaceful."

"Wow," Beth says, her voice once again breathless and quick. "That is weird. I'd hate to work in a place where somebody died."

Steve hugs her, drawing her to him. "But you have been. For a couple of weeks. And you're fine. Really fine." Beth giggles and the warm sound breaks the gloom.

"Are you sure you didn't mind helping us?" Lisa asks, glad to be on another subject. "You gave up a lot of weekends."

"Actually, now I don't know what to do with my spare time," Beth laments.

"There's always more to do," Alan says.

"No thanks." Then, lowering her eyes and flushing a delicate pink, she admits, "I've been looking for second-hand furniture. Redoing the desk was a lot of fun."

Lisa squirms. She put Beth on the desk because she thought

the job was nasty enough to run her off. "You did a beautiful job. I'll bet you wind up with some exceptional pieces."

The redhead beams at Lisa, seemingly unaware of any ulterior motives. "That's what I'm hoping for."

Steve raises his beer in a salute. "Thank god you refinish furniture, not houses. This was fun, but I don't want to spend the rest of my life on remodeling projects."

"Don't worry about that, I'm a confirmed apartment dweller. Especially after this."

The time passes quickly and soon Alan and Lisa are alone again, watching the sun fall below the horizon. Summer had flown by and now the woods are touched with the blazing colors that signal the approach of winter's dark iciness. The corn is brownish-gold, singed by the first kiss of frost. The crisp stalks, so green a short time ago, complement the orange, red and gold of the trees. Husband and wife sit in silence, drinking in nature's palette, aware of each other's closeness, but not touching.

The beauty of the moment, the exhaustion of the last few weeks, the relief at finally getting Alan squared away, or more likely, a combination of the three, causes a tear to slip down Lisa's cheek. Hurriedly, she brushes it away, but not before Alan notices.

"What's wrong, pretty lady?" he asks, one hand tightening over hers. The dam opens up and tears flow in a hot torrent. He draws her close and strokes her hair, murmuring, "Shhh. It's okay. It's okay." The rhythmic movement coupled with his soothing tone calms her down. Alan hands her a napkin and waits.

Without making eye contact she whispers, "I'm sorry. I don't know what's wrong."

"It's okay, you're probably just tired."

She nods. "Maybe you're right. I have been really tired the last few days."

Alan smoothes the bangs back from her forehead. "Recently, our whole focus has been on me and keeping me on track. You've been neglected." This brings a fresh torrent of tears and Alan leaves, returning with a box of tissues.

Lisa takes a tissue and says, "In all honesty, I've been thinking about this whole pregnancy thing." She raises her eyes and Alan flinches at the naked pain he sees in them. She sits up straight and says, "I think I screwed up by waiting too long. I just know I'm not going to get pregnant."

Alan holds her gaze for a few seconds and then shakes his head. "No, sweetheart, you didn't screw anything up. Just because it hasn't happened yet, doesn't mean that it won't. What did your doctor say?" Lisa turns away, tears running down her cheeks, but Alan gently turns her face back to his. "What did she say?" he insists.

She sighs as she exhales. "She said it takes time for the first one. If I haven't gotten pregnant in another year, then we need to look at root causes. Otherwise, I have to be patient." The statement is delivered as if it were a school lesson learned by rote. Alan smiles.

"I see. And you, with all your medical training, know better than she does. So, Doctor Wilcox, what course of action are you going to prescribe? Snake oil? Dancing naked in the moonlight? I'll help you with that one," he adds.

"No," she retorts, trying to hold back a smile, but failing in the attempt. "That's a little extreme. Wait until I get really desperate." Lisa is quiet for a moment and then blurts, "I just want to get pregnant. I'm tired of waiting."

"I'll bet that's going to hurry the process along." Fresh tears threaten and he quickly changes tack. "Come on, sweetheart, why don't you go on to bed? You're exhausted and that's not helping."

Lisa wants to argue, but gives in. He takes her hand and leads her to the bedroom. Once she's undressed and in bed, Alan covers her with blankets in preparation for the cool night ahead. As soon as her head touches the pillows, her eyes droop. Alan kisses her lowered eyelids and whispers, "When you're not so tired, we'll practice baby-making. We'll do it 'til we get it right. I promise."

"Practice makes perfect," she murmurs and drifts off.

10.

The new office is the solution. Not only did Alan's mental block disappear, he was able to make up time in the schedule. Now, on this crisp October morning, Alan is in complete control. His presentation is delivered with such style and confidence that the same people who were neutral two months ago now respond with enthusiastic applause. Even Phil. While his claps are not as loud as those around him, at least he makes an effort.

"What do you think so far?" Alan asks when they have a semi-private moment.

Phil hesitates, then says, "I thought if anybody had a chance of succeeding it would be you."

"Thanks, I—" Alan starts, but Phil raises one long, finely veined hand.

"Let me finish," he says, pausing for effect. He takes a deep breath then continues, "But I didn't think even you could pull this off."

"Why not?"

Phil shrugs and suddenly looks every bit of his sixty-odd years with a couple of decades added on. "I come from an old school of thought and I'm just too set in my ways to change. I thought—think—that employees need daily guidance and—I'll be honest—monitoring." Steve joins the pair, but Phil ignores him, still speaking directly to Alan. "Left to their own devices, people will choose goofing off over work."

Embarrassment creeps up Alan's neck. He hopes the conference room lights, still dimmed from his presentation, are low enough to hide the color in his cheeks. Before Alan has to respond, Steve breaks in. "I've never argued that point with you, Phil. But honestly. What's the difference between Alan working steadily, eight hours a day, five days a week for two months to meet a goal, or if he takes the first month off and works sixteen hour days the second. As long as he delivers, who cares?"

Alan winces at Steve's accurate description. Fortunately, the two managers are engaged in their unending combat and don't notice.

"I care because it is humanly impossible to work that kind of a schedule and still produce quality work," Phil snaps.

"I'm not saying that's what will happen. I'm just pointing out that a person can pull off a sprint. As long as the end results are acceptable you shouldn't care how they're achieved. And besides, once somebody gets used to working without supervision, they learn to pace themselves."

"But until they learn, products will suffer."

"That's no different from training a new employee. Face it. This program scares you because it means you've lost control."

Steve's voice rises and others in the conference room look towards the two men. Phil's body tenses and his hands clench into fists, knuckles white patches against red skin. Neil steps up and puts an arm around Phil's shoulders.

"Gentlemen, we've just participated in an extremely encouraging design review. Let's allow Alan to enjoy his success, shall we?" Neil pauses, but neither combatant breaks eye contact. Neil continues. "This debate on management style, intriguing as it is, can be left to another day. Okay?" The two adversaries glare at each other, the older man still rigid, the younger in a casual stance but betrayed by his heaving chest. "Okay?" Neil repeats, tightening his arm around Phil's shoulder. Neil's voice is louder this time, demanding an answer.

Steve gives in first. "No problem," he concedes, his lips stretched into a humorless smile. "I'm sure we'll take this up later."

Phil shakes off Neil's arm and barks, "Depend on it," and stalks out of the room. It isn't until the man's gone that Alan realizes how quiet the room is. Gradually, conversation resumes and Alan exhales loudly. Neil turns at the sound and claps Alan on the back.

"Don't let it get to you, son. You're just spoiled. Not having to be around these guys is making you soft. I'll bet you go weeks without a good knockdown, drag-out, eh?"

Alan nods. "Oh yeah. This is enough to send me scuttling back to my burrow."

Steve glances at his watch. "Tell you what, since I'm the one who started this mess, how about if I make amends?"

"Why?" Alan asks.

"I'd hate to think your scuttling is my fault, especially on an empty stomach. It's almost noon; what if I spring for lunch?"

"Make it somewhere good and I'll let you buy me lunch, too," Neil offers. With a groan, Steve gives in.

Later, the three push back from their table in unison. Steve adjusts his belt and says, "I always forget how big the portions are here."

"You didn't have to eat all of it," Neil points out.

"But who can resist? This place makes the best garbage burger in town," Alan retaliates.

"Speaking of eating, have you lost weight, Alan?" Steve asks.

"Does it show?"

Neil scrutinizes Alan. "This setup must be agreeing with you."

"It is. I'm not eating as much and I'm walking everyday. I'm not sure who's happier, me, Lisa or my doctor."

"It shows in your work as well," Neil comments. "This is the best stuff I've seen out of you in years. Not that what you did before was bad," he adds hastily. "It's just that what you mapped out today was incredible."

"He's right, Alan," Steve remarks, "You're doing great."

Alan chafes under the deluge of praise and wonders what's next. He doesn't wait long.

"Sorry to beat a dead horse, Alan, but how are you feeling about the schedule? Still comfortable with it?" Neil asks, adding no-calorie sweetener to his coffee and stirring.

Alan thinks about the last two months. For at least two weeks, maybe even three, he'd done nothing. Catching up hadn't been that hard and the results—well they speak for themselves.

Steve jumps in. "What do you think, Neil should we make him an offer he can't refuse?"

Neil nods and Steve leans forward, his fingers coming together to make a steeple. "Here's the deal, Alan. We need this project to come in early."

"We've mentioned this before, but I want to bring it up again," Neil adds. "We believe our main competitor has a similar product. Even worse is that they're on the verge of introducing it. We have to beat them to production or we can kiss this one good-bye."

"If they win this race, it could take us years to recover." Steve's forehead wrinkles as he delivers this announcement. His smile is gone.

"Okay," Alan says, "What do you want? I'm meeting the schedule, the design's going well and there's no reason to believe it won't continue like this."

"This product has the potential to be one of our best sellers, ever," Steve says.

Alan nods, not sure why the obvious is being brought up.

Steve continues. "Neil and I want to extend a carrot. For every month that you bring in the release date, you'll earn a percentage of the predicted annual profits for this product."

Alan stares at his friend for a few seconds and then gazes into his coffee. The inky liquid reflects blackness. Breathing in deeply, Alan looks up. "For every month I pull in the end date, you'll give me a bonus?"

"Right," Neil acknowledges. "A contract'll be written up with the exact amount, but there are a few things to keep in mind." The manager pauses, studying Alan, then says. "For instance, a partial month doesn't count. Chop off three weeks and you earn nothing."

Alan nods.

"Also, the bonus is paid when the product is delivered. If you get ahead in the beginning but then deliver on the original date or later, it does us—and you—no good. Beyond your normal salary, of course."

"Of course."

"Also," Steve says, "If you bring it in enough, we can extend an overall bonus to sweeten the pot. I'm not at liberty to say how much, but it will be worth whatever you have to do to pull it off."

Alan takes a drink of his now cold coffee and winces. He pushes it away and puts his elbows on the table, steepling his fingers under his chin. He meets the collective gaze of the two men across from him and announces, "I'm in. Let's see what we can do."

Steve grins. "I knew you'd go for it."

Alan shrugs. "I don't see a down side."

"That's my boy," Steve says and motions for the waiter.

The next day, Alan looks over the new schedule carefully. He marks the upcoming milestone in red on the calendar, the first week in November. Over lunch, it had seemed easily attainable. Seeing it on the calendar, he wonders what he'd been thinking. That was exactly the phrase Lisa had used when he told her about the change in the contract. Well, almost.

"Are you nuts? The initial schedule was optimistic at best. Now it's impossible."

"Well, thank you for your unwavering support. You can't know how much it means to me at a time like this," he countered.

Lisa was instantly contrite. "I'm sorry, Alan, it's just that it looks like you're setting yourself up for failure." Alan stoked the already blazing fire. The October nights were damp and they built a fire whenever they could. Plus there was something romantic about a fire on a windswept autumn night. Lisa was curled up in a blanket, shivering while she waited for the warmth to build. Recently, she always seemed cold. Alan gave up on coaxing any more heat out of the miniature inferno and joined his wife on the couch. His face softened when he saw moisture shimmering on her face and carefully brushed it away.

"What's wrong?" he asked and drew her to him. He worried about her recent moods; she cried more than she laughed and that just wasn't like her. His flannel shirt muffled her answer.

"Nothing, I'm just tired. And I worry about you."

Alan leaned back on the couch and let her lay down on his lap, still wrapped in the red and black tartan. It felt so good to hold her and stroke her ebony hair. It glowed like a dark ember in the firelight. He could feel her body relax into his arms. "You don't have to worry about me. I know what I'm doing," he assured her.

"Do you?" she whispered, drowsily.

"What's that?" He bent close, trying to make out the tenuous question. But the only sound was her gentle, rhythmic breathing. Alan held her in his arms and let her sleep while he watched the fire burn.

11.

The weekend passes without further incident, even though Lisa is on edge and ready to burst into tears given the slightest provocation. Alan itches to work, but one of his fundamental rules is to keep Saturdays and Sundays free. Unfortunately, Lisa's moodiness is making him rethink that particular rule. By Monday, he's excited to return to the basement.

Alan bends over a scarred workbench. Its addition crowds the office, but, using it, he can solder without burning his oak desk. At the moment he is soldering tiny surface mount components into place. He could have paid to have the boards populated, but the extra cost needed to get them early had blown the budget. Besides, he's very good at this task. Several years before, he'd taken a course in high reliability soldering. He saves money, ensures the end quality and also has fun. Now that the analysis is done, he can do what he really enjoys—build electronic circuits.

Unfortunately, the task is so engrossing that Alan loses track of time. He is halfway through the first board when his stomach growls and startles him into jerking his soldering iron. A resistor no bigger than a grain of rice pops up and disappears onto the floor. Alan swears and starts to chase it, then gives up, realizing it's hopeless. He stretches and notices that it's been hours since he's taken a break. Other than the ring of light cast by his work lamp, darkness shrouds the office. "What time is it?" he asks the hushed room. As if in answer, the phone rings, its shrill cry slicing through the silence. Alan jumps and then snatches the receiver before it rings again. "Hello?" he barks.

"Are you okay?" Lisa's voice sounds distant.

"Yeah—yeah. I'm fine. What's up?"

"It's after seven and I was starting to worry. I came downstairs and knocked but I guess you didn't hear me."

Alan ignores the reproach in her voice. "Sorry, I guess I got carried away."

"Are you coming up for dinner?"

"Sure, I'm starving. Give me five minutes and I'll be right up. Love you," he says and hangs up. In less than two minutes, everything is off and he closes the door behind him.

The only illumination comes from the thin bright sliver under the door at the top of the stairs. The moonless night and lack of streetlights adds to the blackness. Alan flicks the light switch beside the steel door. Nothing happens. "Damn" he mutters. There's nothing between the wall and the stairs, so he steps confidently—and blindly—into the gloom.

Alan moves forward and stops. At first, there's nothing, and then he hears it again. A faint scrabbling noise. He searches the darkness, straining to see. Nothing. He holds his breath, not wanting to telegraph his presence. Suddenly, something slithers across his foot and he jumps sideways, tripping over a carton shoved up against the wall. The overhead light flashes on, searing a starburst into his eyes. Sprawled gracelessly on the floor, he throws up his hands to ward off the light and whatever is behind it.

"Alan, what's going on?" Lisa demands. "You okay?"

Still blinking, Alan brings his hands down. "Yeah," he mutters as he pulls himself up. "More embarrassed than anything. The damn light didn't come on and I tripped."

Lisa stifles a giggle. "When you didn't come up, I got worried."

"You sound worried," he grumbles.

"Really, I am—honest."

"Like I believe that. Come on; make me dinner. I'm starved."

"Okay, but let me go up the stairs first. If you fall again, I don't want to be your landing pad." He smacks her on the butt and she shrieks as she runs up the stairs with him close behind. The noises are forgotten.

The next morning, yawning and balancing a cup of coffee in one hand, Alan makes his way down the stairs. On the final step he pauses, not sure why his skin is crawling. As he scans the open expanse, he sees the light switch by the office door and memories flood in. He flips the switch on his side of the room and the light winks on, sickly green and pale in the morning sun. Alan's heart begins to pound, slowly at first and then speeding up; a miniature jackhammer trying to burst through his chest. The air is oppressive and his breathing is ragged and harsh in the still basement.

Mice, his brain screams, *it's just mice*. But the memory of a scaly body, slithering across his foot, tries to crawl out of his subconscious. Alan pushes it down—down into the special pit reserved for things such as this. Things he doesn't want to think about. Silly things like nightmares about showing up for a design review naked. Or wondering if anyone notices that he can't keep his eyes off Beth. Serious things like whether or not he still pleases Lisa. Fire sloshes across his hand and slices through the errant thoughts. "Son of a bitch," he yelps and drops his coffee cup. It lands on the unforgiving concrete in an explosion of shards and liquid. "Damn it," he mutters.

Grumbling and cursing the entire time, he cleans up the mess and then heads straight for his office, not allowing further distractions. Outside the door he pauses and glances back at the open space. Even though sunlight is streaming in and the light is still on, they are ineffectual at dispelling the shadow scraps clinging to the walls. Panic swells, propelling him towards the door. He jerks it open and runs through, slamming the door and the dead bolt shut at the same time.

Inside the sanctuary he runs a trembling hand over his forehead. It's damp. A laugh echoes through the room, startling him with its hysterical keen. Shocked, he realizes it's coming from his own throat. Desperate for some level of normalcy, Alan clicks on the television. While a talk show rambles on, he puts on a pot of coffee and grabs a Pop-Tart. The caffeine and sugar shoot through his brain, barricading it against the earlier fear. Soon he is immersed in the solid world of solder and components.

The board takes longer to complete than he anticipates and

it's close to nine when Alan leaves the office. The fluorescent light hums softly overhead, exposing his earlier fears as the childish notions they are. There is only one tiny flicker of dread as he starts up the stairs, his back to the wide expanse, and he tells himself that he takes the stairs two at a time because he's hungry. When he wrenches the door open and steps through, Alan tells himself that his heart is pounding because he came up the stairs too fast. By the time the door closes behind him, he almost believes it.

The kitchen is dark except for the light over the stove. A plate covered with aluminum foil sits on top of the counter. Alan lifts the foil and the smell of tomatoes and spices fill the room. His stomach twists and he realizes that he hasn't eaten anything since breakfast. He puts the plate in the microwave and goes looking for his wife.

No other lights are on, so he creeps through the house feeling like an intruder. Once in the bedroom, he can just make out a form under the blankets. A smaller form, curled up at the foot of the bed, purrs loudly in the hushed bedroom. He turns to leave, not wanting to disturb them, when Gandalf stretches and yawns, then tucks his head back under his tail.

"Alan?" Lisa asks.

Alan sits beside her, smoothing the dark hair away from her eyes. "You okay?"

"I got really tired. What time is it?"

"About nine-thirty."

"Mmmm," she says, then becomes very still. Alan thinks she's fallen back asleep but she murmurs, "Did you find your dinner?"

"Yeah, it looks great. Thanks."

"Good." Another pause, then, "Why are you so late?"

Alan kisses the top of her head. "I got caught up in something. Sorry."

"'Sokay. I was good and didn't call," she whispers.

Alan winces and strokes her hair. Impossibly fine and soft, like gossamer. He places a kiss on each closed eyelid and she sighs.

"Go back to sleep, sweetheart. I'll be up in a little bit.

"All right," she breathes, not opening her eyes. He closes the door as gently as he can and head downstairs to his spaghetti.

Sauce had splattered all over the inside of the microwave, so Alan rummages through a drawer, looking for a dishcloth. During his search, he finds the slip of paper that Big Bob had given him. He contemplates the phone number and finally sticks the note on the refrigerator. The spaghetti is looking pretty pathetic, but he's so hungry he could eat the plate. A half container of Parmesan cheese later, it is quite edible.

Friday morning, Alan opens the door to Earl, master exterminator. Alan had expected someone of McClanahan bulk, so the slender, pint-sized man on his doorstep is a surprise.

Earl responds to the startled look with a smile and asks to be shown to the "area of concern." His precise manner, more college professor than bug killer, fills Alan with confidence. That feeling shatters when Earl gives his verdict.

"Mr. Wilcox," he announces with the air of a failed surgeon. "I'm afraid there's nothing I can do."

"I don't understand."

Earl has been kneeling on the floor, examining the baseboards. He stands up; his navy blue slacks and crisp white shirt immaculate in spite of him crawling around on the floor. "Actually, it's good news. I can find no evidence that you have an infestation of any kind."

"That's impossible. There are all these noises and the other night something ran across my foot," Alan insists.

Earl beams a gentle smile and brushes some imaginary dirt off his pristine hands. "So you've said. But it was dark and you didn't actually see anything did you?"

"Well, no, but…."

"And you'd been working late, had you not?" The exterminator strolls towards the stairs.

"Yes, but…."

"When we get tired, our minds—play tricks. The simple truth remains that there are no droppings, I hear no noises and there is no destruction of any kind. Your house is so clean I can't even find cobwebs. You and your wife keep an excellent house."

"Thanks," Alan snaps. "So what's the bottom line?"

"There is nothing I can do because you do not have a problem. As a result, I will not take your money." At the top of the stairs, Earl halts with his hand on the knob, causing Alan to nearly run into him. Lips pursed, the little man says, "I thought you'd be happy."

"I am. It's just that... Well... What have I been hearing?"

Earl studies the man before him as if he is an interesting new species that requires eradication. "I really couldn't tell you Mr. Wilcox. My specialty is the extermination of vermin—real vermin—not things that go bump in the night." With a slight bow, the master exterminator says, "Good day to you, sir," and is gone.

12.

Alan watches Lisa pull her jacket on. The fall colors have been spectacular, but now they are nothing more than drab remnants blanketing the lawn and clogging the gutters. Alan sits at the kitchen table and drinks his coffee while his wife prepares to do battle with nature.

"Sure you don't want to help?" she pleads. "It'll do you good to relax."

"I'll relax when the review's behind me. Besides," he adds with a grimace. "Raking leaves isn't relaxation."

"You're right," Lisa admits as she winds a vivid scarf around her neck, "it's not. But it is good exercise and you haven't done that lately, either. When was the last time you went for a walk?"

Alan scowls into his cup before meeting her worried gaze. His voice is steady, not even hinting at the anger his eyes betray. "Once the review's behind me, I'll walk my damn legs off. Until then, I'd appreciate a little more support and a lot less nagging." Lisa turns her head but not before Alan sees the telltale brightness in her eyes. "What the hell's wrong with you?"

Lisa tugs on a knitted cap and brushes a tear away with one mittened hand. "I can't help it," she says, a sob escaping when she catches her breath. "You haven't been exercising, your diet is awful and I've practically forgotten what you look like."

Alan studies the wind-swept landscape. The sky is leaden, promising more rain as if to make up for the arid summer. He pushes back from the table and goes to her, putting both hands on her shoulders. "Look, I'm trying to find my pace. Once I get it together, we'll do something fun together, even if it's just taking a walk. Okay?"

Lisa nods, her lower lip caught between her teeth. Alan tips her face towards his and gives her a gentle kiss. He can feel her lips quivering under his before she hugs him and presses her face into his chest. Alan holds her tight, wishing he could take a break and help her with the leaves. Instead, he pushes her away with a gentle pat on her butt.

"Go on. You're roasting under all that gear." Lisa tosses him a tentative smile, eyes still bright with the threat of tears, and disappears through the door.

Alan watches it close and then goes through his own door. Once in the basement, he navigates the open area without incident, scanning the corners as he goes. His pace increases with every step. By the time he reaches the office, he is practically running. Once inside, Alan slams the door and it clangs with prison finality. He leans against the cool metal while his heart thuds in his chest.

When Alan's breathing returns to normal, he feels ready for the day. He snags a Mountain Dew, turns on the equipment and begins.

The earlier promise of rain fizzled, replaced by sunshine unusual for late October. The transom window above Alan's workbench brings in light, but the sun makes the room uncomfortably hot. Alan stands it as long as he can, but finally pulls the blinds. Closing off the view is a good move. The sunlit day beckons to him, tempting him to leave the tedious job that shackles him to his bench.

Last week Alan made good progress, but is now stalled. The board powers up but that's it. No blinking lights, no displays, nothing. For days he's tried to unravel the mystery. Eyes closed, Alan traces the design in his head. A tenuous idea appears, but a tapping at the window breaks the thread. He ignores it, but it becomes more insistent. A familiar voice chimes in.

"Hellooo in there," Lisa calls. Mittens cup around her eyes as she peers through the blinds. Alan sighs. He goes to the window and pulls up the blinds.

"What?" he snaps.

"I'm stopping for lunch and thought you'd be ready for a break. How about it?"

"Lisa, I'm right in the middle of something. Can you just leave me alone?" He swears under his breath when he sees the tears welling.

"You have to eat sometime, I just thought maybe we could do it together."

"Not right now. I'll be up for supper. Okay?"

"Sure," she says and moves out of sight. Quickly. Alan thinks about calling her back, but pulls the blinds shut instead. He hesitates for a moment and then returns to work.

An hour crawls by. Alan tries to concentrate, but Lisa's hurt face keeps appearing over his schematics. The solution that had seemed so close has slipped away, possibly for good. Recognizing the futility of continuing, Alan gives up and decides to make amends. He's so preoccupied that he doesn't think twice about crossing the basement area.

Alan throws open the kitchen door and calls, "Hey, pretty lady, what's cooking? It doesn't have to be good, 'cause I'm starving." His greeting echoes back from the deserted kitchen, while his stomach grumbles from hunger and guilt. With an exasperated sigh he wanders through the house, searching for his wife.

The search ends in the bedroom when he finds the shapeless lump under the covers. Alan realizes with a pang that this is how he's coming to think of her. Gandalf looks up to see who's come in, recognizes the intruder and tucks his nose back under his fluffy tail. Lisa doesn't stir and Alan draws the door shut. Within seconds he's at the basement door. He shrugs and goes through.

Lisa opens her eyes, feeling disoriented and groggy. Something has awakened her. She sits up, dislodging a lump that voices his displeasure with an ear-splitting meow. She pulls Gandalf close and cuddles him until he responds with a rumbling purr. With a start she realizes the sun is setting. Even though she's been here the entire afternoon, she still feels tired, as if she hasn't slept at all. A banging noise pierces the fog that envelopes her brain and she realizes that somebody is at the front door.

"Anybody home?" a familiar voice drifts through the house.

Lisa stumbles down the stairs with Gandalf in her arms and

almost knocks Steve over. "What're you doing here?" she asks. Gandalf leaps out of her arms and strolls away as she leans forward to kiss Steve.

He brushes her cheeks with his lips and then steps back. "You look like hell."

"Thanks. Flattery is your strong suit," she mutters, stifling another yawn.

"What I mean is—you don't look like your normal perky self."

The yawn escapes and Lisa moves towards the kitchen. "Well, I don't feel like my normal perky self."

"Are you coming down with something?"

"No, I'm just tired all the time." As she talks, Lisa sets up the coffee maker, putting in half regular, half decaf. This late in the day, she usually drinks just decaf, but right now she needs the caffeine.

Steve frowns. "What does Alan think about this?"

Lisa shrugs. "Not sure he's noticed. Too busy with important issues."

"That's ridiculous." Steve says. After a pause, "Where is he, anyway?"

Lisa shrugs again and reaches for a coffee cup. "Want some?" When Steve nods, she pulls out two mugs and carries them to the counter before answering. "I suppose he's in his dungeon, but I won't swear to it. I'm not allowed to disturb his lordship when he's down there."

Steve's frown deepens. "Well, it's time to disturb him. You invited me for dinner and I want dinner."

"Did I?" Lisa asks.

"Both of you did," he corrects and heads towards the basement door.

"Wait. He can't hear you through the door. Soundproofed, remember?"

"Oh right." Steve thinks for a second and then asks, "Can't we just go in?"

"Dead bolt. He keeps it locked. You know, so he won't be disturbed." Instead of anger, apathy courses through her body.

She wishes Steve would leave so she can go back to sleep.

"Damn," Steve swears. "So how do we reach him?"

"Call him. If you're lucky, he might even pick up."

Steve punches the number into his phone and waits. Alan picks up on the tenth ring.

"Yeah?" Alan barks.

Steve frowns at the object in his hand. "Alan, is that you?"

"Steve? What's up?" The disembodied voice relaxes.

"I was hoping you could tell me."

"What do you mean?"

"I'm in your kitchen with your wife wondering when you're going to join us."

"You're in the kitchen?"

"Uh-huh," Steve says and winks at Lisa, "and if you leave me alone with this lovely lady for too long, I can't guarantee what will happen." Lisa giggles when she hears the expletives ring out just before the line goes dead.

Alan enters the kitchen a few minutes later. He gives Lisa a peck on the cheek and shakes Steve's hand. "How long have you been here?" he asks, opening the refrigerator. "Brewski?" he calls over his shoulder.

"Sure. Not long," Steve adds. "What's for dinner?"

Alan exchanges a glance with Lisa and says, "Sorry, I've been really busy and dinner slipped my mind. How's pizza sound?"

"The works?"

Lisa looks offended. "What else?"

"You're on."

Lisa stays in the kitchen to order while the two men carry their beers into the living room. Steve sits on the couch while Alan builds a fire. A few minutes later a blaze is crackling and Lisa joins them, sipping from a hot cup.

"How's everything going?" Steve asks.

Alan studies the fire. "As well as can be expected."

"Do you think maybe you're pushing too hard?"

Alan's head jerks up. "What am I supposed to do? You're

the one who keeps insisting I move the schedule."

"Wait just a minute. All I did was hand you a challenge. You're the one that's letting it eat you alive. You look awful; Lisa looks worse than I've ever seen her and you don't even seem to care."

"A challenge?" Alan sneers. "That's a laugh. You badgered me until I did what you wanted and now you won't even take responsibility. You make me sick."

Lisa breaks in. "Alan, that's not fair," she says in a tremulous voice.

"Isn't it? I should've known you'd take his side." Turning from his wife to his friend, Alan says, "Is that why you've never gotten married? No woman's ever given you the rush you get from the power of the almighty corporation?"

"Where did that come from?" Steve demands. "I'm worried about you; there's no reason to attack me."

"If you ever stopped thinking about yourself long enough to commit to another human being, you'd understand." Alan is on his feet, shouting down at Steve. The younger man is frozen to the couch, more dumbfounded than angry. "I'm doing the best I can and I am getting no support whatsoever." Before Steve or Lisa can say anything, he storms out of the room.

The slamming door breaks the paralysis. Lisa begins to cry and Steve puts his arms around her. "I j-just d-don't know what t-to do," she sobs. "H-he's always in that d-damned office and I'm s-so t-tired."

Steve rocks her back and forth, murmuring nonsense that calms, soothes. Eventually, she catches her breath and realizes how good his arms feel. She can't remember the last time she's been held. His heart beats against her cheek and she snuggles into the rhythm, relaxing as she feels his fingers touch her hair. Suddenly there's a pounding on the door and Steve is on his feet.

"Uh...." He shakes his head and then tries again. "That must be the pizza."

"Pizza," Lisa echoes and starts to get up.

"No," Steve snaps. Lisa sits. "I'll—uh—get it," he explains and runs to the door, his face crimson. When he returns his complexion is closer to its normal color, but his words tumble out in a rush. "Smells great, want some?" He doesn't meet her eyes.

Lisa nods and hurries to the kitchen to get napkins, plates, and, even though she knows it's useless, tries to call Alan. When the answering machine clicks on, she hangs up without leaving a message. She rejoins Steve and they eat by the fire.

"So," Lisa says, her tone cool and a little distant, "where's your significant other?"

"You mean Beth?" Steve asks, just as cool. Just as distant.

Lisa smacks him on the arm and he grins. She returns the smile, happy to be back on safe footing. "Of course I mean Beth. Who else?"

"I don't know, I got a ton of 'em."

"Seriously, why didn't you bring her?"

Steve takes a swig of his beer. "She went to a chick flick with her buddies."

"Why didn't you go with her?"

"Are you kidding? That much estrogen can be damaging to a real man like me."

"Oh."

Steve puts another log on the fire, causing it to blaze anew. Sitting beside Lisa again, he says, "Can I ask you a question, pretty lady?"

Lisa flushes. "Sure."

"Why don't you ever go out with your girlfriends?"

Lisa stares at her plate. "Because I don't have any." A single tear courses slowly down her cheek.

Steve holds her gaze and says, "I'm sorry."

She brushes away the tear and smiles. "Don't be. I don't have any because I've never wanted any. I always had Alan." Quietly, she adds, "And you."

"Have some more pizza. It cures melancholy."

Lisa takes the offered piece. "I'm serious."

"Tell me something. Why Alan? Why not me?"

"Are you kidding? He saved me from calculus. All you offered was good times." She munches on her pizza, remembering. They'd all struggled through engineering, but Alan had other problems as well. His parents had died the year before he entered college, and tutoring was a way for him to make ends meet. He'd seemed so lost, so alone... Lisa feels herself succumbing to the memory, to the pity, but she shakes it away before it swallows her. "Plus, I wasn't a member of your Beauty of the Month club."

"I wasn't that bad," Steve protests and flips a piece of crust at her. She bats it away and a gray streak pounces on it. Gandalf sniffs at it, and then stalks away, leaving it on the rug.

"Close to it. You had a different girlfriend, each a knockout, every month."

"If you can't have the best, choose wisely from the rest," he quips.

"What's that supposed to mean?"

Steve answers with another question. "Be honest, why did you choose Alan over me? He had to have weighed over three hundred pounds."

Lisa struggles to remember. Alan, quiet, overweight, soulful eyes behind awful glasses. Good-looking Steve, outgoing, athletic, knew where a party or a beautiful girl was, day or night. Then there was her. The third corner of the triangle. She remembered how she'd loved both of them, still did, but Alan had always been there, had always needed her, always loved— worshipped—just her. Still does. *Why settle for being one of the crowd when you can be a goddess?* She shrugs. "Don't know. Never really thought about it."

Steve tips his bottle and finishes it off. "I'd better get going. You look exhausted."

Lisa yawns in agreement and Steve kisses her on the cheek and leaves. After he's gone, she crawls into bed and is asleep in seconds. The only living being that joins her that night is Gandalf.

Steve pauses on the front porch and takes a deep breath. The night air feels sharp after the closeness of the firelit room. He pulls his jacket tight and the movement stirs a lingering scent—

her scent—that's dissipated by the evening breeze. Sighing, he trudges down the sidewalk, feeling lonely and old. *I'll call Beth and see if she wants to come over and keep me company.* He shivers and pulls his collar tight. He knows he'll still be lonely.

13.

Alan stomps down the stairs, his heart and lungs thudding in time. He's never been that mad at anyone before, let alone his best friend. At the bottom he swipes at the light switch and fluorescence illuminates the dark reaches of the basement. Lost in anger, he strides out across the floor. Partway to the closed door, the overhead light buzzes louder and flickers a warning. Alan stops, the back of his neck prickling, and looks up, willing the light to stay on. The other will is stronger, however, and the fluorescent bulb crackles and dies. Alan stands in the middle of the room, blood roaring in his ears. The darkness is absolute and, behind him, the scratching starts.

Panic fills his chest and Alan spins around. Ahead, the noises stop, replaced by scrabblings on either side. His head whips back and forth, as he strains to isolate the source. He decides they are louder on the left and turns to face them, but that direction goes silent. Instead, a cacophony spreads behind him, comprised of claws and scales and even wings slicing through the air. Alan senses slimy tendrils reaching out and he runs headlong into inky nothingness.

He trips on a carton and goes sprawling. His jeans give with a screeching rip and warmth trickles down his leg. On hands and knees, he scrabbles forward, a pathetic echo of his pursuers. Without warning, his head smacks into concrete and he's driven backwards. Colors explode and a ringing fills his ears, deafening him. Something cold oozes across his hand and he shrieks.

Repulsion spurs him into action. He staggers to his feet and, swinging his arms as he moves forward, he finds the wall. Edging sideways, never leaving its firm presence, Alan follows it to the left. He reaches a corner and turns, touching drywall, ever mindful of the noises gaining on their prey. The terror is suffocating and he moves faster, rational thought gone, only raw instinct left to guide him. Just as he is convinced they will overtake him, he feels the door knob. Dizzy with relief, he leaps to safety, slamming the door behind him. He falls to the floor and lies in the now welcome darkness. The only sound is his gasping breath.

After a while, he's not sure how long, he pulls himself up and turns on the light. Protected by the radiance, he stumbles to the refrigerator and locates a beer. He pulls the tab with trembling fingers and gulps half of it in one swallow. He drains it in another and reaches for a second. By the third he's feeling almost human. Carrying the rest of the twelve-pack over to the couch, Alan stretches out and clicks the remote. Six beers later, he's snoring peacefully, the television blasting away unwatched and uncaring.

The sunlight is intolerable. Alan sits up with a groan and rubs his pounding temples. The pain stops long enough for him to stand, but then a new, sharper agony tears through his body, forcing him back onto the couch. Gritting his teeth, he examines his knee. The ripped jeans are caked with dried blood. Memories rush back and he gags on the sour taste that fills his throat. Staggering to his feet, he runs to the bathroom.

The porcelain sink feels good under his feverish hands. He leans against it for a few seconds then finds a bottle of aspirin. He swallows three, letting the water flow as he strips off his ruined jeans. Jaws clenched, he grabs a washcloth and scrubs at his knee. The blood dissolves to pink rivulets in the sink; psychedelic spider webs slung across the porcelain. Thinking about spiders makes Alan's skin crawl and he scrubs harder, scraping the fear away.

By the time the wound is clean and bandaged, the pain has dulled. Alan splashes water on his face and then studies the reflection in the mirror. Blood-shot eyes peer back at him. The dripping face, unshaven and ghastly, is unrecognizable. "What's happening to me?" he mutters.

After drying off his face, Alan wanders into the living area, the television still blasting away. "Repent," it screams. "Forgiveness is there for the asking."

"Amen to that," Alan mutters and clicks it off. The last of the twelve-pack beckons, but common sense wins out and he goes to the door. He pauses, thinks of how childish this is, and twists the handle.

The basement is empty, the fluorescent bulb buzzing in the morning sunshine. Frowning, Alan flips the switch and the bulb winks out. Again and it's on. Alan's throat tightens, the familiar pounding starting in his ears. "Stop it,' he demands. The command bounces off the uncaring walls and settles into his spine. He steels himself and begins the interminable journey across the floor.

Halfway to the stairs, he notices a dark stain on the concrete. His knee throbs at the memory of the fall. He traces the maroon splashes to the wall, around the corner and to the door. His stomach lurches at the thought of remaining long enough to clean up the mess. He tears his eyes away from the gruesome trail and scurries out of the basement.

The smell of coffee fills the kitchen. Alan pours a cup, ignoring his trembling hands and glances at the clock. He jumps. It's after eleven. He goes in search of Lisa.

This time he heads straight to the bedroom. Several layers of blankets make it hard to tell where the bed ends and Lisa begins. Alan sits on the edge of the bed and shakes the pile. A muffled groan escapes from deep within. "Morning," Alan says.

"What time's it?" Lisa asks; face still buried in the pillow.

"A little after eleven."

"God," she mutters and rolls over, rubbing her eyes with her fists and yawning. "I was up for a while but then...." Her face clouds over. "You okay?"

"I'm fine," he assures her. "I need to call Steve."

"He's worried—so am I."

"Don't be," Alan counters, irritation tingeing his voice. "Next week I'll be fine. For better or worse," he adds.

"Next week?"

Irritation wins out. "Design review? My paycheck?"

Lisa stares out from her cocoon. "I'm sorry, I knew it was

coming up but I wasn't sure exactly when. It's not as if you talk to me anymore."

Attrition replaces irritation. "Tell you what, as soon as I get the prototypes done for my presentation, we'll go out to eat. Okay? Somewhere special. You pick."

Lisa smiles and lifts her arms to him. "Okay," she whispers.

Alan gives in to Lisa's warmth, ignoring the moisture trickling down his neck. He can't think of anything he'd rather do than spend Sunday with her.

Alan is making excellent progress. There's no reason he won't be ready for the upcoming design review. Occasionally, Lisa's weird moods creep in and distract him, but he forces them away, just like the stained concrete. He keeps meaning to clean it up, but hasn't had the time. At least, that's the line he's taking.

The day goes well and he quits earlier than he has in a while. The sun is just starting to set as he leaves the office. He turns on the light and starts across the basement. He stops in mid-stride. Something is different.

Puzzled, Alan stands in the middle of the room. Suddenly he realizes what has changed and he runs up the stairs, two at a time, his breath coming in short, harsh gasps. Lisa is in the kitchen making supper when he bursts in.

"This is a surprise—," she begins, but Alan won't let her finish. He grabs her by the shoulders, his fingers clawing at her flesh.

"Were you downstairs?" he demands.

"Yes, I…"

"Did you see anything? Hear anything?" Each question is punctuated by a shake.

A tear rolls down her cheek. "No, n-nothing," Lisa stammers. She pulls away and falls against the counter. She straightens her blouse and says, stronger this time, "Nothing except for that awful stain. Is it blood? Where'd it come from?"

Alan stares at her. "It's nothing. You had no business cleaning it up. It was my mess; I was going to take care of it."

"Alan, what's going on?" She's angry now, matching him.

Tears are still rolling down her cheeks, but she wipes at them absently. Staring him down.

"Nothing. Promise me you won't go down there alone, okay?"

"That's ridiculous. Why not?"

"Just promise me, damn it. Can't you ever do anything without a freakin' inquisition?" His voice is rising, but he doesn't care. Doesn't care that his wife is staring at him like he's lost his mind. Maybe he has.

"All right. All right..." Lisa scrubs at her face with a bedraggled tissue.

Alan yields. Drags his hand across his face. Takes a deep breath and tries to slow down his thudding heart. "I'm sorry," he says, but Lisa looks doubtful. Wary. He touches her arm and she shrugs it off. He grabs her hand. "I'm really sorry. I'm just on edge," he explains and pulls her to him. Hugs her. She's stiff in his arms. Alan breathes in deeply. "What's cooking?"

Lisa becomes very still and then slumps. "Uh, kind of hard to tell." she says, pulling away and wiping at her face.

"Mind if I take over?" Alan asks as he rummages through the cabinets.

"Sure," she says and steps aside.

The sun is trying its best to break through the clouds, but the clouds are winning, enveloping the windswept day with a seething leaden shroud. Alan tingles with excitement. It's a day for headless horsemen and hounds that roam the moors.

"That smells heavenly," Lisa says, interrupting his musings. He turns from the window and they kiss.

"Cinnamon rolls, fresh from the oven."

"How long have you been up?"

Alan waves at the pan. "Long enough to pop these babies out of the tube and into the oven. Coffee?"

"Sounds great," she says and sits down.

Alan brings two mugs, setting one in front of Lisa and carrying his to the other side of the table. The brew warms him all the way to his stomach. Rain drums against the windows, making the room cozy. Alan looks across the bleak fields and thinks of moors. Lisa grimaces and sets her cup down.

"Something wrong?" he asks, tasting his to see if it's all right. Seems to be.

Lisa shakes her head. "I'm not sure; it's not sitting well." She pours it out and sits back down with a glass of milk. "Much better," she announces, after a tentative sip.

"I've been beat out by Elsie," Alan says and rolls his eyes mournfully.

This elicits a giggle, but it doesn't last. Her face is serious when she asks, "What time did you come to bed last night?"

"I'm not sure."

"I really don't like this. Except for breakfast I never see you anymore."

"Just be patient a little while longer," he begs and starts into the same old line. "Once this milestone is behind me I—" Alan stops in mid-sentence and snaps his fingers. "I almost forgot. I've got news for you, pretty lady."

"You're quitting your job and taking up something less stressful—like bomb squad detail," Lisa suggests.

Alan ignores the dig. "The circuit's working. I'm going to make it with a few days to spare."

"Are you serious?"

"As a heart attack. Listen, how about a celebration? Somewhere nice."

"Where?"

"Anywhere you want. Think about it and let me know when you get home from work."

"Work?" Lisa echoes, then glances at the clock. "Oh, my god. I'm late." She shoves back from the table and rushes out of the room. She comes back just as quickly and kisses him on the lips. "Love you," she breathes and is gone. Alan sits in the snug room and enjoys his coffee, savoring the taste and feel of her soft lips on his.

Alan whistles as he walks across the stretch of concrete to the office. Once in, he slides the dead bolt home, no longer noticing the comforting 'snick' that locks the rest of the world out. The morning drizzle has given way to sunshine that fills the room with a golden haze. The tension of the last few weeks is a gray memory, just like the earlier rain. He flicks on his computer and gets a Mountain Dew out of the refrigerator. Balancing the icy can in one hand, he picks up his cell phone and sees that he has messages.

Voices float past but one catches his attention. "Yo, Alan, pick up. Huh. Okay, I realize you set your own hours now, but this is ridiculous." Alan glances at this watch. 10:00. Damn. The voice plows on. "Anyway, this is John, the best damn purchasing agent in the world. Okay, maybe in the universe. Give me a call. Pretty important." A click and the next message starts.

Alan cuts off the stream of messages and dials John's number. The phone is answered on the first ring. "Speak," barks a voice. Once Alan identifies himself, John swings immediately into the crisis. "You know the amplifiers you ordered? Well, they're on allocation."

The simple phrase brings Alan's stomach into his throat. Allocation means exorbitant prices and impossible lead times. "What can we do?" he chokes out.

"You've got two options. Wait six months and hope you can get the parts, or design in another component. And I gotta tell ya, unless you're willing to sign a Faustian contract or give up your first born, I wouldn't count on six months."

Alan rubs his forehead. "I promised full production in four months."

"Then you've only got one option."

Alan doesn't remember finishing the conversation or hanging up the phone. His mind is already creating, and rejecting, modifications. Nothing looks promising. For the first time since he's started on his own, he misses having a sympathetic ear. Alan leans back in his chair, hands behind his head, sorting through possibilities. Sunlight pierces his eyes, causing him to lose his balance and fall over backwards.

"Dammit," he rages to the empty room.

He's rearranged the furniture several times, but the window has become a constant irritation. As it is, it shines directly into his eyes. If he turns the desk, it reflects off the monitor. Blinds and curtains do little good and besides, Lisa has been using the window as a door bypass. Alan chews his bottom lip as he scans the room. After a few minutes he jumps into action.

A couple of hours later, Alan scrutinizes his handiwork. After stuffing the window with insulation, he's covered the opening with drywall and spackled the cracks between it and the existing wall. Once the plaster dries, he can sand it down and paint it. No one will ever know a window existed. When he has time, he'll fix the outside, but for now, this will do. An added benefit is that the construction, loud and growing worse every day, is blocked out. As the houses are completed, families will move in, bringing kids that play in the street and make all kinds of noise. Removing the window was the right thing to do.

Several hours have been lost, but it's worth it. The insistent light on the cell phone reminds him there is one more distraction to deal with. He turns off the little phone and shoves it in a drawer. Irritants gone, he takes a deep breath and begins. It's going to be a long weekend.

The Potting Shed is even more crowded than it had been in the summer. The patio is closed and its summer occupants, the plants that comprise the mini-rainforest, moved inside. Although the place is filled to capacity, it seems there are more trees, bushes and vines than there are customers. Lisa doesn't mind because it feels like a tropical island. A boisterous, crowded tropical island, but enjoyable nonetheless. Even a sociable fichus tree tickling her neck doesn't ruin the mood as she and Jessica tackle bowls of chicken gumbo. The spicy fragrance blends deliciously with the aroma of fresh baked bread tucked cozily beside the soup.

"I'm not sure where we're going," Lisa says. "Alan says it's my decision."

"Make sure it's someplace expensive."

Lisa takes a hesitant sip. So far the soup is staying down, but she doesn't want to push her luck. She looks at Jessica with a slight smile playing around the corner of her mouth. "Don't you realize we're not dating anymore?"

"What's that got to do with anything?"

"Everything. The money is not his and mine, it's ours. Besides, I'm having a hard time deciding. My stomach is in a constant uproar these days."

Jessica frowns. "Are you still tired all the time?"

"Yeah. That's the other thing. I don't know how late I'll be able to stay up." Jessica smiles with a patronizing smugness that makes Lisa bristle. "What?" Lisa demands.

"Aren't you trying to get pregnant?"

Realization dawns. "Oh my god," Lisa squeals. The occupants of several nearby tables look up, but they're ignored. "With everything going on, I hadn't even thought about it. Wouldn't that be wonderful?"

Jessica reaches across the small wooden table and squeezes Lisa's hand. "Yes, it would be," Jessica murmurs. "And I couldn't be more happy than if you were my own daughter."

Lisa takes a deep breath. "Well, don't go buying diapers just yet."

"But all the signs are there. Promise me you'll call when you know for sure," Jessica demands.

"I will, I promise. Right after I tell Alan."

"Oh fine, put me second. It's not like he had anything to do with it." The two laugh as they finish their soup.

14.

Lisa drives carefully to avoid the trick-or-treaters darting from house to house. As she eases into the cul-de-sac, the children's cries fade with the houses. One house isn't worth the effort, so their street is ignored. The thought saddens Lisa but only for an instant. Soon there will be houses with their own trick-or-treaters. Maybe young enough to play with her little one. She pulls into the garage and sits for a minute, resting a hand on her belly.

Humming under her breath, she strolls into the kitchen. "Honey, I'm home," she sings out. The only sound in the dim emptiness is the ticking clock. Glancing at it, Lisa realizes it isn't even six yet. Still humming, she skips up the stairs, clutching a brown paper bag.

The bag's contents tempt her, but she resists the seduction. She's waited this long; a few more hours won't hurt. Alan should be there when she administers the test. Resolve intact, Lisa undresses and turns on the shower.

When Lisa steps out of the shower and into the bedroom, she frowns at the numbers glowing in the dark, 6:20. Unease prickles along her neck. "No," she proclaims to the empty room. "Nothing is going to ruin this evening." A chill passes over her body, forcing her back into the bathroom's steamy warmth.

After putting on her make-up, she decides not to ruin the effect with glasses and pulls out her contacts. The struggle to insert them draws tears, which destroys her previous work. Ten minutes is spent repairing the damage, but the end result is worth it. A stranger sparkles at Lisa from the mirror. She laughs and skips into the bedroom.

A few minutes later, Lisa catches her breath as she studies the looking glass belle. Her blue silk dress shimmers as it clings to her voluptuous body, accentuating every curve. The outfit is Alan's favorite and thinking of his reaction makes Lisa shiver with anticipation. She scans herself one more time and smiles. The workouts are paying off after all. *Not for long*, she giggles and tries to picture herself with a swollen belly. Finally, she breaks away from the mirror and totters down the stairs on unfamiliar heels. She picks up a novel lying by the couch and waits.

Impatience frays Lisa's nerves by the time the clock chimes eight. "Where the hell is he?" she demands of Gandalf. He stares at her, not bothering to answer. Lisa turns back to her book but can't pick up the story line. She can't remember the last dozen pages. Finally, no pretense at being calm, she slams the book down and makes her way into the basement.

Lisa shivers as she hurries through flickering shadows to the office door. The overhead light is dim and buzzes fretfully. Halfway across the expanse, she catches movement to the right. She snaps her head around, but—nothing. Her pace quickens to match her heart and she reaches the door in seconds. The knob refuses to turn so she pounds on the door. No answer. All she does is bruise her fists. "Oh hell," Lisa mutters. She marches back up the stairs and swipes at the light switch, plunging the basement into darkness. She's so angry she doesn't hear the claws scrabbling across the cement.

Back in the kitchen, her head feels as if it's about to burst. She snatches up the phone and pokes out Alan's number. When the voice mail clicks in, Lisa stifles the urge to scream. Instead, she hisses "Where the hell are you?" and snaps off the phone. She paces back and forth, until a window catches her attention. *Of course.*

The morning's light drizzle is now a vicious downpour. The umbrella hinders more than helps because of the wind. Focused on her mission, Lisa slogs through the deluge, ignoring the damage to her silk dress and heels. "Alan had better have a good excuse," she mutters through clenched teeth, "like he's lying unconscious or dead."

Once around the corner, Lisa fights through the bushes and swears as a branch catches her hose, ripping fabric and skin in one swoop. She works her way to the window that opens into Alan's office and stops. Where there should have been light there is—void. She taps on the glass, softly at first, then harder. Suddenly, the glass gives way and pieces fly. In the dim light, she sees blood well up on the side of her hand. Chilled to the bone, she disentangles herself from the shrubs and trudges back to the house, wrapping her hand with the skirt of the now ruined dress.

In the upstairs bathroom, she strips off the silk dress and dumps it on the floor. The ruined hose and shoes follow. The naked caricature in the mirror mocks her while she removes her contacts. Lisa steps into the shower and cries as the water beats against her skin.

Every joint in Alan's body creaks as he stands up. The effort was grueling, but successful. The replacement part isn't as good as the original, but it will do. He strolls to the refrigerator and pulls out a Mountain Dew. His optimism has returned and he knows he's going to make it. He can't wait to tell Lisa.

Lisa. What time is it anyway? Alan drinks the soda without tasting it. He'd worked for a while and fallen asleep on the couch, but not long. Of course, if it was really late, Lisa would've called him. She hadn't, so no problem. He looks for his phone, but it's not on the desk.

Suddenly, a memory rattles through his cottony brain. With shaking hands he pulls the phone out of the drawer, the light blinking accusations as Alan rings voicemail. The first few messages he skips but then a familiar voice, almost unrecognizable with rage, begins. "Where the hell are you?" it spits.

Alan closes his eyes and rocks back on his heels, hands laced together behind his neck. "I'm so sorry," he whispers. Opening his eyes, he looks at the equipment crouched on his workbench. "But will you believe me?" No answer. Bracing himself, he yanks open the door.

Ancient, terrible blackness greets him. Alan claws at the switch, but nothing relieves the gaping emptiness. Sweat beads on his forehead. He can't stay here. He thinks of calling Lisa then dismisses the idea. Even if she answers, she'll think he's lost his mind. Alan stands in the doorway overwhelmed by the desire to scuttle back to safety. *But Lisa...* The longer he stalls, the more trouble he's in. *God, what am I going to do?*

The stairs are only twenty feet away, mere seconds really, but the distance stretches out like eternity. While fear paralyzes him, rooting him to the doorway, a faint breeze touches his cheek. He flinches away from the foul caress and suddenly it's as if the basement has expanded, as if a door has opened. With intuition born not of experience or education, but from that deep inner self that remembers cowering before a fire and listening to animals howl in the jungle, Alan knows that he needs to leave. Now. *Now...* He licks parched lips and forces his leaden feet to carry him into the unknown.

After a few steps, the office door slams shut, snatching away the small circle of light and leaving him in total darkness. Blood pounds in his ears and his legs feel as if they are plowing through molasses. His outthrust arms push through the gloom, clearing the way. As he struggles forward, the hideous din he remembers from before swells all around. In spite of protesting lungs, he wills his legs to move faster, hurtling through the dense emptiness. A bone jarring collision with a wall stops his mindless rush.

Dazed, he falls back onto the concrete. Tomorrow—*if you have a tomorrow,* a voice gibbers in his head—aches and bruises will flourish. Now, the pain is unnoticed as he scrambles to his feet. Flailing to find something, anything, stable, his arms crash against the railing. He lurches onto the stairs, sobbing in relief and terror. Slimy tendrils brush against his forearm and snake around his ankles as he stumbles up the stairs.

On his hands and knees when he finally reaches the landing, he throws on the switch and light explodes like an atomic bomb. Gasping, Alan looks past the black starbursts and scans the basement. *Nothing.* The area between the stairs and the office is bereft of anything, good or bad. Confused, Alan takes a step forward. As he stares, fear takes over and he retreats to the kitchen. He wipes his forehead with his sleeve and it comes away soaked. As he closes the door, he makes a mental note to put a flashlight, a big one, in his office.

Alan starts towards the bedroom, expecting to find Lisa. On his way, he notices a fire crackling in the fireplace. Its warmth beckons and he feels as powerless as a moth being sucked into a blazing candle. So mesmerizing is it that he almost doesn't notice Lisa sitting on the couch, hypnotized by the same flames and stroking a rumbling Gandalf. She doesn't move when he sits down beside her.

"That feels nice."

"I see you've decided to join the land of the living."

A dank breeze strokes his mind. The fire throws off some of the chill, but it is deep in his bones. He may never be warm again. "Did you build that by yourself?"

"I had to. There was no one else around," she says.

"Look, I'm sorry I missed our date. Something came up."

"For two days?"

Alan winces. "I know this is hard, but if I'm going to make this work, I'm going to need—" Lisa cuts him off before he finishes his sentence.

"What you need. What you need… I am sick of hearing what you need. What about me? Do you ever think about me anymore? Do you ever think of anyone but yourself?"

Alan's tone is conciliatory but with an angry undercurrent. "Just calm down. It was only one night. I'll make it up to you. I promise."

"And just how are you going to make it up to me? Do you have any idea of what I went through last night trying to get in touch with you? Trying to talk to my husband?"

Alan shakes his head, his anger dissolving before her searing torrent.

Lisa rages on. By now she's off the couch and stalking around the living room. Gandalf flees to safer—saner—grounds. "I tried knocking on your fortress door—"

"Did you come into the basement last night?" he demands,

his voice trembling slightly.

She rounds on him. "Yes I did. It's my house too and I can go where I damn well please." Alan isn't listening. The thought of claws scratching against the concrete nauseates him. "After that I called. In my own house I tried to call my husband. But he didn't answer."

Lisa's voice is dim and far away. *Lisa was down there with those things. Alone.* And he wouldn't have been able to hear her. Couldn't have helped her. Couldn't have saved her. *God.* He faded back in.

"Do you have any idea how humiliating it was to crawl around in the bushes trying to get your attention? Do you?" Her face is white except for two splotches on her cheeks and her hands are balled into tight fists.

"I'm sorry," he says. She stares at him for a moment, an emotion close to hate blazing out of her eyes, then shakes her head and turns to the fire. Alan gazes at the bowed head and feels an unbearable agony filling his throat and chest. It is hard to breathe. He waits as long as he can and then wraps his arms around her heaving shoulders. She throws him off but he embraces her more tightly than before. She struggles but he doesn't let go. It lasts forever but eventually she quits fighting and relaxes, her body curving into his, sobs fading.

Alan turns her face to his and kisses her damp cheeks and eyelids. He brushes the bangs away from her forehead and kisses it too. Murmurs cascade from his lips. Neither he nor Lisa know what he's saying, but neither cares. He rocks her back and forth, the crackling fire the only sound in the room. Alan's shirt sticks to his chest, damp with tears. "I'll make it up to you," he murmurs.

"You can't," she says with a sorrow deeper than the rage of a few minutes—a few eons—ago.

"Why not?"

"I was going to," she hesitates, searching for the right word, "discover something with you, but now we can't. I know and you'll never be able to find out with me.

"Sweetheart, you're not making sense."

"I'm pregnant," she whispers, so low he almost doesn't hear her. Then, understanding dawns and he can't breathe again.

"You're pregnant?"

Lisa nods, tears threatening again. Alan crushes her in another embrace and then draws back. "Did I hurt it?" he asks, suddenly frightened—terrified—by what he has done.

In spite of herself, Lisa smiles. "No, you didn't hurt it." Her face becomes solemn. "But you did hurt me."

"Yes, yes I know. I'm a brute, a jack ass, I don't deserve to live," Alan says, the words tumbling out in a rush.

"You're not that bad," she says, tenderness creeping back into her voice.

"It doesn't matter," he says, holding her at arms' length. "Don't you get it? I'm going to be a father," he beams. "A father, me."

Lisa grins along with him. "Yes and I'm going to be a mother."

"That's right. They go together, don't they?"

"Now you're just being silly," she says, laughter skipping in and out of tears. Alan jumps off the couch.

"Have you eaten anything?"

"No, not really."

"I'll make Fettuccine Alfredo ala Wilcox."

"Is that Italian?"

"No, it's delicious," Alan says with a grand flourish and a deep bow. "I think I can even dig up all the makings for a cheesecake. You're eating for two now—you need a lot of energy."

Lisa follows him into the kitchen. "I don't think that's the kind of energy I'm supposed to have, but since it's fettuccine—and cheesecake…." Alan bustles around while Lisa hops up on a barstool. "So what happened to the window?" she asks.

Alan thinks for a moment, trying to remember, then tells her everything—almost everything—that happened.

15.

Thanksgiving comes and goes and Christmas is bearing down like a juggernaut. Alan peers at the wipers beating against the windshield, just barely keeping ahead of the snow. He turns up the heat and glances at Lisa. The bucket seat is all the way back and she's asleep, snoring softly. Her doctor said the fatigue is normal and will pass after the first trimester, but it's easier to deal with now that they know. His conscience still prickles when Alan realizes how much Lisa had changed without him noticing. The exhaustion, the mood swings, the nausea, any one should have set off an alarm, let alone all three. *God, she'd been what, four weeks pregnant before we realized it? And that's only because that dike friend of hers, Jude or Jess or something put two and two together.*

Alan takes a minute out of his self-recrimination to peek at his wife. She's so beautiful. The short hair that he'd criticized so harshly (another prick of guilt) gently frames her face. She shifts, trying to find a comfortable spot and her mouth parts slightly, a trickle of drool shining on her lower lip. The drop makes her look vulnerable. Alan wrenches his gaze back to the icy road and concentrates on getting them to her parents in one piece.

Lisa's friend was the only one to point out the obvious. Since then, Alan's attention is focused where it should have been all along, on his wife. Neil and Steve aren't happy about it, but they're getting what was promised in the beginning. Schedules will be met, bills will be paid, but, best of all, he's going to be a father.

Lisa stirs and wipes at her mouth. "Where are we? The North Pole?"

"Yeah, sleeping beauty, I decided to take a detour and pick up our presents early."

A beautiful smile appears. Everything she does is beautiful. *She's the mother of my child.*

"I like what you did with the window. It doesn't look too bad from outside."

Alan doesn't ask which window. He knows which one.

Lisa watches the landscape sweep by. "The trees look sugar coated... I think holidays up here are always more Christmas-y —because of the snow," she says and then shivers.

"Do you want me to turn up the heater?" Alan asks, reaching for the knob.

"No, father hen," she says. The tears are mostly gone, replaced by familiar laughter. "I'm fine. Just excited. Anyway, are you sure you want to keep the window covered up?"

"Definitely. It was a distraction and it was only going to get worse."

"Hmmm... I still don't like it, but at least you're not locking the door anymore." She pauses and then, "Alan, why were you so upset when I went into the basement?"

He shrugs. "That was stupid of me. I thought there were mice or rats or something down there and I had the crazy idea they would hurt you."

"Did you call an exterminator?"

"Uh-huh," he says, watching for the exit. Visibility's down to less than twenty yards and he doesn't want to miss it.

"What did he say?"

"Who?"

"The exterminator." She sounds impatient.

"Sorry, got my hands full. Uh—he said you're a good housekeeper, but no vermin."

"That's a relief. Did he know what he was doing?"

"Seemed to." Alan peers through the snow, trying to make out landmarks. Everything looks strange, festooned with cancerous growths. He frowns. "He's an interesting guy, reminded me of a college professor. Name's Earl."

"Dr. Earl, Professor of Things That Go Bump in the Night?"

Alan glances at Lisa, his skin crawling. "It's weird that I hear noises, but haven't found anything. Him either."

"Did you try another exterminator?"

"I was going to, but then the noises just stopped. I haven't heard anything since—let's see—I guess it's been since after I found out you were pregnant."

"Huh. Now that's weird."

"I know. I haven't been down there as much, but I'd think that'd make it worse."

"True—watch out," she cries.

He jerks and the car slides to the left. Still shaking, Alan regains control and gives her a questioning look.

"The exit," she explains, pointing to a barely visible road sign.

The urge to tear into the silly woman swells then subsides. Now is not the time to turn on the water works. He relaxes his clenched fists and eases onto the exit ramp. Lisa chatters on about Jess while Alan reigns in his churning thoughts.

As predicted, Lisa's parents were ecstatic. Her father pressured them into staying through New Year's and Lisa and her mother went shopping almost every day. They bought so many things for the baby's room that most of it had to be shipped home. Alan listened to Lisa and her mother prattling on about the stuff and tried not to think of escalating bills. Her parents offered to pay for everything, but Lisa wouldn't let them.

Now they're home again, ready for their familiar routine. Lisa's mother calls every day, which really helps Lisa. Alan wants to help, but he doesn't even pretend to understand what she's going through. His contribution is to stay accessible. Door unlocked and phone on. His work is going well and the year promises to be the best one ever.

Alan thinks about all these things as he moves around the kitchen, putting water on to boil. Pasta sounds great. Over and over, *I'm going to be a father* runs through his head like a stuck record. He laughs. His child won't know what a record is, let alone a stuck one, and for the first time in a long time, he doesn't feel old. He needs one of the big pots from the pantry, so, whistling under his breath, he heads for the garage. When he opens the door, Lisa's car makes him frown. The expression remains as he goes in search of his wife.

Lisa is curled up on the couch, holding Gandalf in her lap. The room is dark; she hasn't put on a light.

Alan's frown deepens. "What are you doing home?"

Her eyes never meet his, her hands never quit stroking Gandalf when, in a voice as frigid as the room she announces, "I started spotting today."

16.

Beth runs into the condo with Steve close on her heels. After hours on the slope watching her snake back and forth, he can't wait to get her out of her suit and into the hot tub. He catches up with her just inside the foyer. She tries to twist away but he traps her wrists in one hand and pins them over her head.

Steve closes his mouth over hers, parting her lips with an insistent tongue. She turns her head, but he twists his fingers into her auburn hair, pulling her lips back to his. A moan escapes and she becomes still, no longer resisting. The fragrance from the cedar planks mingles with her spicy scent and he can hear her rapid breathing, feel its hot touch on his cheek as he kisses the base of her neck. Steve's free hand lightly traces a path down her throat, continuing to an outthrust breast, made sleek and firm by the emerald Spandex. His need grows, and he releases her wrists, sliding down to cup her buttocks instead. With one motion he sweeps her up, her legs wrapped around his hips, and buries his face between her full breasts. This time the moan comes from Steve as he thrusts against her, frustrated by the thin fabric that keeps them separated.

"Steve—honey—hold on, okay?" The voice comes from an incredible distance. Steve fights to clear the stupor that binds him and Beth laughs a rich, throaty laugh.

He steps back, letting her feet touch the floor, and frowns. "What's wrong?"

"We're meeting Bob and Kris for drinks, remember?"

The frown deepens. "You mean that broker and his floozy we met at brunch?"

Beth slides out from under him and moves towards the bathroom. "The rich, heavily connected broker and his expensively bejeweled floozy," she corrects. "I have plans for you my dear and we need all the friends we can get. Especially ones with connections." Steam fills the bathroom. Steve enters, strands of blond hair darkening from humidity.

"Here's a crazy idea. Let's forget ambition for just one night and stay in. Just you and me. I'll build a fire, we'll drink some wine and stay in the hot tub until our fingers shrivel into prunes."

"Oh, that's sweet, but you never know when a break'll come. There's plenty of time for you and me later."

"Okay, but it's barely six-thirty. Don't we have time for—uh —you know…." He hates to be reduced to this, but he's only human.

The giggle slices through him neatly. "You silly, there's barely enough time for me to get ready as it is. My make-up and hair alone take over an hour. I have no idea how I'm going to dress in half an hour."

"Your make-up looks fine. Hell, you spent an hour this morning putting it on."

"That was my morning face. Now I need my nighttime face. Be a dear and fix me a glass of Chablis, okay?"

Steve delivers the wine and then pours some whiskey. Standing on the balcony in the icy Colorado night, he sips his drink and waits for the ache to dull. He looks at the stars, searching for answers but finding nothing.

Three whiskies are annihilated by the time Beth is ready and they head for the lodge. The place is packed and Steve doesn't think they'll find their new friends. His hopes are crushed when Beth squeals and drags him to a crowded table. There's a lot of jostling and laughter as room is made for the newcomers and they squeeze in between sweaty partiers. Steve orders another whiskey and lets the prattle flow over and through him. It's many hours and twice as many drinks later before he can pry Beth away.

The ride back to the condo is subdued, Steve concentrating on the road, Beth humming the last song they'd heard before the lights had come on, signaling closing time. Kris wanted them to come and finish the party at their place, but Steve begged off. Beth argued but gave in when she realized he wasn't going to budge. Now she hums, her head on his shoulder, her arm tucked under his.

"Do you ever get tired of all this?" Steve asks. His voice is harsh, scraped raw from yelling over the lively bar scene.

"You mean do I ever get tired of having fun? Hardly."

"No, tired of spending time doing nothing with people we don't care about."

"Jeez, you're a bundle of laughs. What brought this on?" she demands, sitting straight up, no longer leaning against him.

"I dunno. I guess I don't have much to show for my life."

"What else could you possibly want? There are people who'ld kill for your life."

"Maybe... But I want more." Spruces whip by the SUV, black sentinels standing guard in the gleaming snow. Beth hunches down in her seat, arms crossing her chest.

"Ever thought about having children?" Steve asks, still staring at the road.

Beth's sneer doesn't have to be seen; it's an entity in the suddenly icy interior. "Oh my god, is that what this is about? Now that your little friends are procreating, your life is meaningless?"

Steve sets his jaw. Silence reigns for a small eternity and then Beth starts chattering about the people at the lodge. There's no need for him to join the conversation, which is fine.

His mind drifts to how the evening will end. A soak in the hot tub with a glass of wine followed by a session in front of the fireplace. Thinking of Beth lying bare-assed on the rug makes him tingle. He shoots her a quick glance and grins.

She smiles back and says, "That's better," and links her arm in his. She leans against him and he can feel her heat through the layers of clothes he blames for the sweat trickling down his back. A strand of hair, soft and fragrant with musky spice, tickles at his mouth. Steve blows it away and her lips brush against his cheek. A promise of what the night will bring ...

"Whatcha thinking?" she asks.

Steve squeezes her thigh. "Actually I was—"

"Oh look," Beth shrieks, her fingernails digging past his flannel shirt and into flesh.

He can just make out the condo and what had to be a dozen cars, trucks and four-wheelers parked in front. A large group of people mills around and their laughter can be heard over the rumbling engine. A pain shoots through his jaw and he realizes he is grinding his teeth. A deep breath and he asks, "Beth, what the hell is going on?"

Beth turned to him, eyes shining. "Isn't this great? Kris was so bummed when I told her you didn't want to go to their party that she must have brought everyone here."

Carefully, Steve asks, "Did she think of this on her own, or did you nudge her just a bit?"

"Uh—well—umm—I might have suggested—something. I really don't remember."

Steve eases into a space in front of the condo, trying to avoid the revelers. At this moment, he doesn't care whether he misses them or not. "You knew I wanted to come back and relax." A pause. Deep breath. "I wanted to get some sleep before hitting the slopes tomorrow."

"I'll sleep when I'm dead," Beth quips as she jumps out of the truck. A welcoming cheer follows her up the sidewalk to the door.

Steve remains behind the wheel until the last person files into his condo. Finally, he yanks the key out of the ignition and trudges inside. The party is in full swing—these are obviously professionals—and the noise level is ear-splitting. Steve winds his way through the bodies and heads for the bedroom.

The room is pitch black, so the light created by the opening door acts like a spotlight. A spotlight aimed at young love. The girl uses her hands, ineffectually, to cover heavy breasts while her companion snaps, "What the hell're you doing? We were here first."

Steve rubs his temple. "This is my bedroom and what I'm doing is going to bed."

"Oh," the boy says, his brusque gallantry dissipating.

The girl chimes in. "We aren't doing anything. We're just talking. Honest," she explains and gathers her clothes.

"Don't worry about it. I'm leaving," Steve says and pulls

the door shut. Behind it there is a burst of giggles, then silence.

17

February is the dreariest month of the year. Alan sits at the kitchen table watching the rain fall for the fourth day in a row. He's convinced the sky will never be blue again. The cornfields, vibrant not that long ago, are dead stalks jutting from dead earth. Snow would be nice; anything to hide the hopelessness.

Thinking of snow dredges up Christmas. *How could we have been so happy then and so miserable now? Of course, it's mostly February's fault. This stupid month doesn't even have a good holiday.* Alan sighs and takes a deep swallow of his coffee. Once he thinks of Christmas, the rest follows relentlessly.

A blighted ovum. The doctors don't know what causes it, don't know how to prevent it, but there it was. By the time Lisa was finally admitted for an ultrasound, she was no longer just spotting, but bleeding, heavy, sinister, black blood. The doctor's pronouncement was anticlimactic, a mere confirmation of what everyone already knew. There was nothing. No dead fetus, no snuffed life, just—nothing.

With a detached air, the doctor explained that a fertile egg divides into two parts, a placenta and a fetus. In some cases— Lisa's case—only the placenta develops. After the first trimester, her body realized its mistake and purged itself. There was no pain, no D & C, nothing.

Alan rubs his hand across his eyes. There is no closure, no ending. *Nothing.*

Unable to handle the thoughts any longer, Alan's mind blanks and he watches rivulets form on the windowpanes. Several of them meander together and form a mini-river. As he watches it flow, a forgotten memory creeps into his brain. Within seconds Alan is descending into the basement.

The overhead light is losing ground against the darkening corners, unable to penetrate the murky patches that cling to the walls. Alan retrieves a flashlight from his workbench, its beam strong against the darkness. He feels armed, secure. "That's stupid," he announces and immediately regrets his bravado, like whistling in a graveyard. The echoing words send a chill down his back. He shakes off the feeling and walks to the wall.

The rain reminds him of Lisa's comment about the basement leaking. If it is, that explains the strange happenings. The dank smell, the light bulb shorting out, even the noises can be attributed to seepage. Alan remembers a Florida vacation and seeing water bugs as long as his thumb. They clustered around streetlights, dull gray with three-inch wings and inch long claws. The bugs had made the same clicking noises he'd heard in the basement a few months ago. He's never seen any around here, but maybe some have migrated. A new kind of alien invasion. Down on hands and knees, he inspects the base of the wall for dampness. A noise on the stairs causes him to whip the flashlight around, nearly blinding Lisa.

"Watch it," she says, holding her hand before her eyes.

"Sorry," he says, scrambling to his feet. "I'm looking for leaks."

"Why?" The question is flat, not caring if an answer comes.

"You thought our foundation might be leaking. Remember?"

"Did I?" she asks in the same listless voice.

Anger flares. The crying was awful, but it was nothing compared to this faded imitation of life. "Yes, you did," he insists.

"Mmmm."

"For god's sake, will you snap out of it?"

"Snap out of what?"

For the first time since she's entered the basement, hell, for the first time since—it, there's a spark of emotion. "This funk you're in. I'm hurt, too, but I'm dealing with it." The words are harsher than he intended, but it's too late. They crackle in the dead air. Lisa crackles back.

"How dare you?" she hisses. "You can't possibly understand the pain I'm in."

Alan steps backward.

"*I* was the one who felt the changes. *I* was the one who

thought I had a living, breathing child in me. Instead, it was a lie. A vicious, evil lie." Lisa steps towards him, fists clenched.

Her anger pushes Alan back even further. "Okay," he chokes out, "you win. You hurt more. But sometimes things just happen. We have to get past it."

Lisa barks a short, unpleasant laugh. "You just don't get it, do you? I'm too old. We're too old." The words stab and slice. "We waited too long. There will be no little Lisa, no Alan Junior, no family; just you and me, sweetheart."

Alan stares at her, horrified by this person, this stranger that has invaded his life. The poison she's spewing both frightens and infuriates.

"You make me sick," he snaps. This time Lisa steps back and it's his turn to vent. "Do you think this is the first miscarriage in married history?" She opens her mouth but he rushes on. "This happens to lots of people and they keep trying. They get on with life," he says, his voice almost a scream.

Lisa shrinks back, pale and beaten, tears welling up. "You don't understand," she whimpers.

This time he does scream. "Yes I *do*." The words echo around the basement, ricocheting against the walls until they wink out. "I was going to be a father. And now it's gone, gone, gone." A fist slamming against the gray uncaring wall punctuates each 'gone'. A bright red splotch marks the last slam.

Lisa sags, sobbing loudly. Alan storms into his office, the only sound louder than the door clanging shut is the dead bolt slamming home.

Alone in the basement, the fluorescent bulb buzzes and then goes black, plunging the room into darkness. A low creaking, like the sound of rusty hinges being forced open, cuts the silence. A few seconds later, a musty fog billows along the floor. The cloud dissipates quickly but an evil chuckle lingers for quite some time.

"Hey kiddo." Jessica pulls up a chair and flops into it. Lisa stares, no—make that glares—long enough that Jessica, who's backed down CEO's with the mere twitch of an eyebrow, begins to feel nervous.

Lisa's eyes flit to the window and she says, "I really don't have time to talk, Jess. I'm pretty busy."

Jessica's eyebrows arch as she takes in the bare desk and the dead monitor in power saving mode. "I can see that."

Lisa flushes. "What do you want?"

"I want what everybody wants," Jessica replies, back in control. "I want you to climb out of that pit you dug for yourself and get back to your old self. The company needs you." She scrutinizes her friend. Smudges, like purple half moons, curve under Lisa's eyes. In a soft voice, strange for her, Jessica adds, "And I need you."

The dam breaks and tears spill down Lisa's cheeks. She pushes back from her desk and stands against the window, head bowed and shoulders heaving. Jessica moves to Lisa's side and puts an arm around her. She can feel the stifled sobs vibrating through the slim body.

"I just can't get it out of my head," Lisa wails. "There was n-nothing. Nothing."

Helplessness surges through Jessica. "What does Alan say?"

Lisa's head snaps up, rage sparking from her eyes. "It wasn't inside him."

"True, but isn't he grieving just as badly? You should be leaning on each other." Defending Alan, a man, feels odd. Jessica doesn't like it. She shakes it away and refocuses on Lisa who's talking again. Or rather, ranting.

"Have you been talking to him? Sneaking around behind my back?"

Jessica fights the urge to run. "Are you two talking?"

Lisa avoids Jessica's eyes. "No. All he does is work. He even sleeps in that damn office."

Searching for safe ground, Jessica asks, "How's that going?" A bitter laugh tells her that she needs to keep looking.

"Great. Just great. Without anything to distract him, like me or a baby, he thrives." Lisa chews on her bottom lip and then adds. "He shaved a week off the schedule. He'll probably get some kind of medal or something."

"Do you think he's throwing himself into his work to get his mind off what happened?" Jessica says, struggling to keep her voice non-judgmental.

"Excuse me," Lisa says and resumes her place in front of the computer. She types, her fingers a blur, and never even glances at her friend.

Jessica stands for a short while and then shakes her head and leaves, easing the door shut behind her. Once in the hallway, she leans against the wall and inhales deeply. The life flowing around her is a striking contrast to the death residing behind the door. *Poor Alan. If I were married to that little wench, I'd lock myself in the basement, too.*

A young man runs up and gasps, "Germany's on the line. They're demanding to know why the new interface is only in English. John and Mike are both gone and I don't know what to tell them."

Jessica forces a smile. "Lead on, dear boy. The Calvary's on the way." Matching him stride for stride, Jessica retreats to Germany.

Alan hooks up the power supply. His soldering has improved with each board until the latest ones are quite good. This one is the best yet. He's made some alterations, and, if this board works as well as the simulations, power consumption will be down by thirty percent.

Eager to see the results, Alan flips on the power. The current meter pegs and he snaps the switch off. Too late. Half a dozen traces peel up. "Damn, damn, damn," Alan shouts.

Alan glares at the smoking mess and knocks his chair over as he stands. He paces back and forth. "Dammit," he rages. He can't handle another delay. Before the bills had piled up— Christmas, the baby stuff ('*money well spent*,' a voice croons), the house, his equipment—the bonus had been a nicety. Now it's a necessity; the only way out of the pit he's dug.

He'd already cut out a week and was anticipating another two. To make that happen, the new boards were ordered with a two-day turn. The cost was exorbitant, but worth it.

Unfortunately, the flu had ripped through the PCB house, taking out half the staff. They'd returned his premium, with apologies, and delivered the boards a week late. Now, after two days of soldering, the board is ruined. A howl rips out of his throat as he throws back his head, fingers tearing at his hair until his scalp tingles.

Abruptly, he snaps his mouth shut and disentangles his hands. He grins. "Couldn't have done that at corporate." Still grinning, he grabs a beer. "Definitely couldn't do this," he mutters and takes a deep swig, refrigerator door still open and cold air billowing into the room.

Hmmm. A case minus two. Twenty-two beers. Don't want to be cut short. Good thing the store delivers. God knows I can't ask Lisa to make a run. Grimacing at the thought of his wife, he grabs some chips and throws himself onto the couch. Beer in one hand, remote in the other, bag of chips on his lap, he relaxes. *Too tired. That only leads to more mistakes. Better to stop and get an early start tomorrow.*

Nine beers later, Alan searches for something to watch. *Nothing. Damn.* "A thousand channels and nothing but reruns," he announces, his voice thin and whiny in the empty room. He looks at the clock. 1:07 A.M.

After a few minutes listening to an idiot selling a portable grill ("And that's not all you get," the salesman chirps, baring his teeth in a shark-like grin), an idea materializes. Alan sees his flashlight on the counter and grabs it.

"Aha," he crows, brandishing the flashlight like a sword. He's pleased that his voice is now strong and confident. "Just a leak and some waterbugs. Yeah." He slices the air with his light. "En garde beasties," he cries as he pulls back the bolt and ventures into the basement.

The light shines overhead, but Alan knows it's untrustworthy. As predicted, halfway across the floor, a familiar buzz announces its death. Heavy clouds obliterate the full moon and the basement is plunged into jet-black nothingness. Alan stands in the center of the room and strains to hear. Just as he is about to give up, a faint scrabbling begins off to his left. Nerves tingling, he waits. He grins into the darkness as a staccato rhythm beats in his chest.

After what seems like hours, a new sound appears. A loud clicking, claws raking across stone. Orienting to the sounds, Alan slowly brings up his flashlight. The noises don't falter. Either they can't see him or don't care. Alan focuses on the spot the flashlight will illuminate and flips it on.

The light is more intense than he anticipated. Spots blossom on his retinas and he's blinded. He rubs his eyes with his left hand and holds the light with the other. Claws rake across his outstretched hand in an explosion of pain and he drops the light. The tinny sound of breaking glass informs him that his weapon is useless. In a panic he turns and stumbles back to the office, praying that he's not turned around.

Scaly fingers grab at his ankles, making him run faster, arms splayed out ahead of him. He runs into the wall full speed, his hand throbbing from the impact. A howl, not even close to human, shrieks out of his throat. Gibbering, he falls against the wall and sidles crab-like along its surface. Slimy tentacles caress his body as he scrabbles for the door.

Just on the brink of falling into madness, his groping fingers make contact with the knob. He sobs as he wrenches it open, light from the office piercing the blackness. Behind him, the overhead bulb flicks on, echoing the warm radiance that brightens the empty space. *Empty.*

Alan's heart slams against his rib cage, blood roaring in his ears. Nothing but boxes and smooth walls. *Impossible.* He draws his hand across his forehead and shakes, wondering if his sanity, along with everything else, has deserted him. A flash of color catches his attention. Three parallel tracks snake along the back of his hand, drying, but oozing purple-black in some places. He gags and the bitter taste of digested beer floods the back of his throat. Choking it down, he backs into his office and bolts the door.

After bandaging his hand and downing two more beers, Alan

lies on the couch. The pounding in his chest has faded, but he can't relax. When he does eventually drift into a fitful sleep, his dreams bristle with claws and fangs and slime.

18.

Lisa drives home in a downpour. The weather matches her mood, gray and cold. The drive isn't long, but it forces her to think and she doesn't want that right now. What she wants is to brood but an inner self is growing stronger, rejecting the self-pity that she's been nurturing for the last month. This strange self sounds like Jessica even though they haven't talked in over a week. Lisa scowls as she navigates the treacherous streets. Jessica's nothing but a busy body.

"Don't you think he feels grief, too?" The question beats in time with the wipers. Anger and sorrow collide, and she's blinded by an onslaught of tears. Headlights glare and Lisa swerves back into her lane, a horn blasting in her ear. She takes a quivering breath and grasps the wheel with both hands, knuckles white, fingers clenched. *It isn't fair. Jessica's never been through this. She doesn't understand.*

As she drives, fighting to keep control, a new question joins the wipers. *"Are you angry because she's right?"* Lisa closes her mind to the voice, but it persists. *"At least you can get out of the house. Be with people. Alan's trapped."* Guilt tickles in her stomach, begging for attention. She pushes it away, as deep as she can, but it's like holding a beach ball under water. Just when she thinks it will stay, it slips out of her grasp and bounces back up to the surface, overblown and gaudy, impossible to ignore. She cranks the radio and concentrates on the road.

Once home, Lisa pours a glass of wine. She downs it in three swallows. A sourness lingers on her tongue but she can feel the liquid work its way through her body. The voice mellows. She pours another glass and takes slightly more time to drink it. "Who cares?" she asks the empty kitchen. "Not Alan."

This revives the voice. Sounding more and more Jessica-like, it observes, *"Oh, you mean he doesn't care about you the way you've been caring about him?"* Lisa chugs the third glass and the voice retreats once more. Bottle in one hand and glass in the other, she wanders upstairs and turns on the television. The glass is too slow, so she puts it aside, drinking straight from the bottle.

Lisa isn't sure what time she fell asleep (*'passed out,'* the *Jessica voice whispers*), but her pounding head wakes her up around six. Something digs into her side and she pulls it out, wincing at the empty wine bottle. Fighting the urge to throw up, she pulls on a robe and stumbles in search of coffee and aspirin.

Twenty minutes later both drugs are working their magic and she feels almost human again. A mist is falling on the gray landscape, softening rather than drenching. Lisa opens the patio doors and lets the fresh breeze wash across her face. She closes her eyes and breathes in the smell of damp earth. The day hints at the spring to come. Lisa smiles. The corn will be up soon and Alan will watch its progress day in and day out, reveling in the cycle of life. Alan. He's locked himself away and Jessica claims it's her fault.

"Is it true?" Lisa demands of the near-spring day.

Something whispers, *"You know the answer..."*

For the first time in ages, a tear falls that isn't for herself or her never child. She closes her eyes and rests her forehead against the glass. A few more tears join the original, but there aren't many. The time for tears is past. Now it is the time for moving on, for forgiveness. *Alan has to forgive me. He simply has to.*

Voicemail answers on the first ring. The message is old, full of the life they used to share and it gives Lisa hope. Her message is short but—she hopes—convincing enough to persuade him to come upstairs. She considers going down in person, but knows what will happen. Instead, she builds a fire in the family room. Flinging herself onto the couch, she contemplates the flames and waits for her husband.

Lisa is asleep and there's nothing left of the fire when Alan trudges into the room. He shakes her into consciousness and she nearly shrieks. He's lost weight just as she's begged him to, but it isn't a healthy change. The man standing in front of her is haggard, bags under eyes that dart here and there, checking out every corner, every shadow. She isn't completely sure, but his hair seems grayer. It's difficult to breathe.

"What d'you want?" he demands.

Lisa sits up and smiles. Filling it with all the love she has. "I want to apologize."

"For what?"

"For not being there for you. We should work through this together." Alan's eyes snap to a movement in the corner. Gandalf strolls out of the darkness and Alan relaxes. Lisa's spine prickles. "Did you hear what I said?" she asks.

"Uh—yeah—yeah, sure," Alan says, constantly scanning the shadows.

Anger builds, cleaner than self-pity, but still not useful. She holds it in check. "What are you doing?"

His searching eyes finally settle on her, but they look through her, not registering her as real, or maybe—as not dangerous.

The anger fades. "Alan, you're scaring me. What's going on?"

He drops onto the couch, propping his elbows on his knees and burying his head in his hands. "I'm not sure," he mutters. "There's something in the basement."

Lisa giggles. Alan jerks his head up and she covers her mouth with her hand. Even though the situation is odd, it feels good to laugh again. "I'm sorry," she says and puts her arms around her husband. "I'm not laughing at you."

"No?"

"No. I'm not. It just sounds like a campfire story. You know, the ones that make you stay up all night, afraid to go to the outhouse even though you're ready to burst?"

His face relaxes. Not a smile, but not the scowl that was there seconds ago. "It does sound kind of stupid, doesn't it?"

The band around Lisa's heart loosens a bit. He doesn't look

that bad after all. "Yes it does. But it's not surprising."

"Really?"

The plea makes Lisa ache. She gives him a quick squeeze. "Really. It's just mice or something and you've built it up into something bigger, more mysterious." Lisa warms to her subject. "You've been working yourself to death and I've been pining away like a kid that didn't get a bicycle for Christmas."

"Was that what you wanted?" Alan asks. His face is serious, but his eyes are living again. "Next year you can have one with a banana seat and streamers. Pink."

Lisa answers with a pillow against the side of his head. Alan catches the pillow and squeezes her hand. Tightly. Returning the squeeze, Lisa pulls him off the couch towards the basement. "Come on."

Alan resists at first, but finally allows her to drag him along. "Where are we going?" he asks, the wary look returning to his eyes.

"To the basement," Lisa calls over her shoulder. "To show you there's nothing there."

"Of course not. Not with two of us," Alan explains as he follows her down the stairs.

In spite of her brave demeanor, apprehension pricks at Lisa. She shakes it away, and pulls boxes away from the wall. "Where do you hear them most?"

"Over there," Alan says, pointing to the far wall. "I think there's a passage."

Lisa studies his face for signs of teasing. Nothing. She walks to the wall and feels the rough surface, avoiding a dark smudge about chest high. Nothing. It's damp, but solid. Not even a hairline crack. She looks back at him.

"I know they're here. Look," he says and pulls back his sleeve. "One of them did this." Three angry welts snake down his arm. One oozes greenish-white pus.

Nauseous swells into her throat. "When did that happen?"

"The other night. The light went out while I was looking for them and something scratched me in the dark."

"Are you sure you didn't hit your arm against a box or

something?" Lisa can't tear her eyes from the gashes.

Alan shakes his head, but without conviction. "It's possible." He studies this new idea, and then says, "But I know I heard something."

"Tell you what," Lisa says. "I'll call an exterminator. Okay?"

"Okay."

"Great. Now, since we're down here, show me what you've been working on."

Alan glares at the computer screen, not seeing the numbers that dance across it. He should be happy but he isn't. After their talk, Lisa has returned to her old self. They even made love that afternoon, something missing for months. They both avoided discussing the miscarriage and life seemed normal again. And it is. Except for the basement. The latest bug killer found nothing but a quick way to make forty bucks. Now Alan sits and stares at the screen, trying to figure out what to do.

It's obvious that Lisa doesn't believe him. She probably told the guy not to look too hard since she doesn't believe there's anything there. Alan's brows come together. *Why is she sabotaging the creatures' extermination? Unless she wants to get rid of me. Whether they kill me or drive me nuts, what does it matter? I'll be out of the picture.* He shakes his head and stands up, pacing up and down. *That's crazy. She loves me—or does she? Maybe she blames me for the baby. Maybe—maybe there's someone else.* Suddenly the office feels hot. Confining. He has to get out. Alan hurries through the basement and is gone.

Everything looks foreign to him. For the past few months, his whole universe has shrunk to the office. The freedom is intoxicating and he lets the car drift along with traffic, unsure of where he's going and not caring. For the first time in ages, he has all the time in the world.

A half-hour later he's staring at a mall entrance. A group of teenagers push past, giggling and talking, oblivious to the old man staring at them in wonder. *Was I ever like that?* Exhaustion weighs him down. His euphoria evaporates, leaving him questioning the decision to leave his sanctuary.

"Oh well," he announces. Two women pass, frowning and picking up their pace. Alan laughs and it brings back some of the good feeling. "In for a penny..." and he pushes into the alien world.

An hour later, Alan drives home, the back seat full of packages. One of them rustles now and then. He feels great. Back in control.

It's tough juggling the boxes down the stairs, but Alan makes it without damaging anything. Food, a cage, and—Huey. The bored girl in the pet shop assured him that the ferret can take care of any small critter that might be lurking. Alan releases the animal from its cage and watches it glide along the wall, predatory eyes bright with the thrill of the hunt. *The girl was right. The little guy'll make short work of the varmints.* Satisfied that the problem's solved, Alan leaves Huey to his work and returns to his.

No longer distracted, Alan is able to work. Really work. Things progress so well, in fact, that he quits at four to surprise Lisa with dinner. The last time he'd cooked for her was before the miscarriage. In a different life. Whistling, he closes the door and steps into the basement. *I'd better put some food out for my new friend,* he thinks, walking towards the stairs. The sun is still up, but shadows are lengthening, hinting at the coming night. That's why he doesn't see Huey until he slips on the blood.

Alan lies on the floor, dazed by the impact. He puts out his hand to push himself up and feels something squish. Close scrutiny reveals it's Huey's intestines, which are spilling out of his mangled body. Alan turns his head and throws up as black spots dance before his eyes. He starts to put his head between his knees, but that will bring his face too close to the stinking pool of carnage. Instead, he staggers to his feet.

The ferret's sleek fur is dull and matted with blood.

Something had torn out his insides, which now lie scattered around his body. Blood pools in a fetid halo and the stench of swamp water and gore fill the air. Alan leans against the wall and vomits again. Even though it adds to the foul aroma, it clears his head. *This has to be gone before Lisa gets home,* he thinks, and runs to the kitchen.

It doesn't take as long as he thought it would to clean up. The hardest part is the vomit. It resists his attempts to mop it up, sliding in a nauseating fashion. He continually stops and turns his head to breathe, pushing away the queasiness. Finally, it's in the bag along with Huey's mutilated corpse and a ton of soaked paper towels. The rest of the ferret's belongings are stuffed into a second bag. Luckily, tomorrow is trash day, so by tomorrow night all evidence of the grisly slaying will be gone.

He's setting the two bags on the curb when he freezes. *What if the bag rips open? Is it legal to throw dead animals in the trash? Worse, what if somebody—Lisa—thinks I killed Huey?* Panic and indecision battle for a few seconds, immobilizing him. But then… *The rest of the stuff's fine, but I'll take care of Huey. He deserves a private grave.* Alan grabs the bag and a shovel from the garage and heads for the cornfield.

Dusk is falling by the time he's buried the hapless animal. His chest is tight and sweat pours off him in spite of the cold. He's still queasy from finding poor Huey. Alan turns his face to the sky and a gentle breeze dries the sweat. The tightness fades, but not the nausea. He gathers his tools and heads for the house. The windows are dark, the half-closed eyes of a brooding monster that crouches and waits. *For me.* As he stands in the gloaming, a thought slides into his head. *Huey was attacked during daylight. Not only do the creatures kill; they're not confined to darkness.* Alan studies the house, reluctant to enter its maw. Rain begins to fall, washing away all traces of Huey's passing.

19.

Steve looks out his window onto the beautifully manicured lawns of Benton International. The ancient oaks epitomize the dignity and grace of a more sedate era. Usually the view is calming, but today he doesn't see it. A discrete knock draws his attention.

"Got a minute?" Neil is standing just inside the office. The project manager motions to the door. "I knocked but I guess you didn't hear me."

"Sorry, my mind was—um—somewhere else."

"I can come back another time," Neil says as he sits down.

"No. No," Steve protests. "Now's fine. I can use a distraction. What's up?"

"I hope you can tell me." Neil's tone is too casual, revealing unusual tension. "What's going on with Alan?"

Steve's stomach performs a lazy somersault, kicking bile into the back of his mouth. He swallows hard, trying to get rid of the bitter taste, but fails. He answers with the same tone of unconcern. "I'm not sure I understand the question."

"Don't play games, Steve. Alan just cancelled the design review indefinitely. He's citing personal problems."

Steve is hypnotized by a tiny bubble of spit balanced on Neil's lower lip. The bubble is amazing, holding its shape in spite of the contorted surface it sits on.

"Since you're his best friend and champion, I figured you can explain what's going on." Neil's mouth clamps shut. The bubble pops.

Steve shrugs. "I haven't talked to Alan in a while. I know the miscarriage tore Lisa up and I assume it did the same to Alan." A new expression replaces the anger in Neil's face. Steve wants to rub it in, but doesn't. He does regain his composure, though. "I can talk to him. Find out where his head is."

Neil relaxes. "That'd be great." He pauses and then, "You

know, I don't want to sound cold, but Alan was going great guns. It'd be a shame if he misses out on the bonus."

"Yeah, but that's life."

"And our butts."

Steve nods.

On the way out, Neil pauses, "What were you thinking about when I came in?"

"Nothing in particular."

"Don't give me that."

Although Steve doesn't know him that well, Neil seems like a good guy. Lost without Alan to confide in, Steve confesses, "It's Beth."

"Nice girl. What's the problem?"

"Nothing really. We have a great time together, like the same people, enjoy the same things." Steve rattles off the list by rote. "She's beautiful, smart, good career, good future...."

Neil's eyebrows rise. "Sounds awful. I repeat, what's the problem?"

"The M word."

A deep laugh explodes from across the desk, making Steve jump. "Sorry," Neil says, still laughing. "You poor guy. You must be terrified."

"It gets worse," Steve admits. "She's going on about kids. Lots of them."

This time the laugh doesn't catch Steve off guard even though it is, if anything, louder than before. "Run. Run as fast and far as you can."

"That's the really scary part," Steve counters. "I'm not going to run anymore."

Neil shakes his head. "A sad, sad day. The passing of an era." In a serious tone, the laughter gone, he says, "Honestly, Steve, it's the best thing that could happen to you. Especially with a woman as great as Beth."

Steve nods. "I agree. Even the kid part. I've always wanted children and I'd like to have them while I'm young enough to enjoy them."

Neil sticks out his hand. "I'm glad you told me. Good

luck."

"Thanks," Steve says, gripping the hand.

At the door, Neil pauses. "You'll let me know what you find out about Alan, right?"

"Sure." And Neil is gone, leaving Steve with the gray February landscape.

Everything he'd said is true and he's close to proposing. But... *How can I ask Beth to marry me if I can't even say I love her?*

"Hello?"

"Lisa?"

"Steve. Hi." She can't remember the last time they talked. It's great to hear his voice. "What's up?"

"It's been a while and I want to invite myself over to dinner; maybe tomorrow night?"

"Sure! Is Beth coming?" Probably her imagination, but Lisa swears there's a hesitation.

"No, she's busy."

"We can make it another night."

"No," Steve barks. Then, an apologetic laugh. "Lining up schedules is tough and I really want to see you guys."

"Okay," Lisa says as she works her way down the basement stairs. "I'm heading towards Alan's office. Of course, he hasn't left the house in weeks; I can't imagine an objection." She reaches the door and knocks. No answer. She tries the doorknob with the same lack of success. After knocking once more, she gives up. "Still there?"

"Yeah."

"He's not answering. I'll talk to him about it and if there's a problem, I'll call you back. If not, assume we're on for—oh—how 'bout seven?"

"Sounds great. I'll bring wine."

After Steve hangs up, Lisa dials Alan's number. She's relieved to get him and not voicemail. She truly hates technology.

"Alan Wilcox, may I help you?"

"I'll bet you can, hot stuff."

The distant voice warms by several degrees. "What can I do for you, pretty lady?"

Lisa laughs. "For one thing, you can open the door and let me in."

The temperature plummets. "Where are you?"

"Outside the door."

There's a clatter and the door flies open. Alan shoves Lisa against the wall and scans the open area. Then he grabs her by her shoulders and shakes her. Hard.

"What the hell are you doing down here?" he yells.

Lisa tries to keep her voice steady, but fails. "Steve wants to come for dinner tomorrow night," she says and swipes at her cheek. "I said it was okay."

Alan isn't paying attention. Instead, he peers into each corner, again and again. After one final scan, he grabs her by the elbow and hauls her up the stairs. At the landing, he wrenches open the door and shoves her into the kitchen. The phone drops from her hand and batteries scatter everywhere. She shakes him off.

"What is wrong with you?" she demands, rubbing her arm.

His face is mottled and he's breathing in short angry gasps. "I told you not to go down there alone," he barks. "Why don't you ever listen to me?" He stands a foot away, legs spread, nostrils flared. The odd mixture of maroon and white in his face are frightening.

"Because you're not making sense. There's nothing down there; the exterminator didn't find anything."

"No, he didn't," Alan says, the sudden calmness worse than anger. "And I know why."

Lisa swallows against a parched throat. "Why?"

"Because it's nothing he's ever encountered before."

"What?"

Without answering, Alan grabs her arm again, bruising it, and pulls her into the family room, looking over his shoulder the whole time. Once there, he lets her go and she loses her balance, falling onto the couch. "Stay there and I'll build a fire. We need heat."

Tomorrow there will be bruises shaped like fingers. Right now, it's inconsequential. Lisa waits in silence while he builds a fire.

When the fire is roaring, Alan sits down and clutches her hands. His eyes are feverish, but at least his color is normal. The fire feels good against her chilled skin. "I've been thinking about this for a long time," he begins. "Recently, I've been under a lot of stress which caused bad feelings. You know, anger, tension, whatever."

Alan looks to her for a response. Not understanding what he wants, she nods. That seems to be right because he continues.

"Normally all those negative emotions are dissipated by coming home, seeing people, going out, whatever. But since I've been working here at the house, there's no outlet and the emotions are concentrating in the basement." Alan jerks to the left, sees nothing and turns back. "That ugliness is a beacon. Calling to the creatures; allowing them to open a gate, a-a portal if you will, between our world and theirs." He takes a deep breath. "When anybody else comes into the basement, the negativity scatters and the signal's broken. The creatures return to their dimension and leave nothing behind except maybe a rotten smell, like swamp water."

Finished, he waits. Panting slightly like a dog. Lisa stands and walks to the fireplace. Picking up the poker, she stabs at the flames and watches sparks twist and turn, like her thoughts. A faint memory—a fetid breeze caressing her cheek—struggles to manifest itself but fails, fading like a will-o'-the-wisp. She shakes her head. "That's pretty outrageous, sweetheart."

Alan's shoulders sag. He silently pleads for understanding. Begging for assurance that he isn't alone. "What about the scratches?" He rolls back a sleeve, revealing puckered scars.

Lisa wants to reassure him, but can't feed these fantasies. "Anything could have done that. But I doubt it was creatures from another dimension." She fights to keep the emotion out of her voice, but it's hard to mask her feelings.

For a second, Alan looks as if he's about to cry. Then, he

snaps his fingers. "Huey!"

"The duck?" Lisa asks. Bewilderment is taking over.

"No. No, a ferret," he explains. "I bought a ferret to hunt them, but they got him first."

"Uh-huh."

"No, really," he protests. "I did."

"Okay," she says slowly. "So where is it?"

Again, he deflates and the momentary animation drains away. "I buried it." He pauses and then adds, "I was afraid you'd think I did it."

Lisa doesn't say anything. *Which is worse? Imaginary creatures killing an imaginary ferret? Or him—my husband, the one I love—killing a living, breathing animal?*

Alan rubs his forehead. "I threw out the food, the cage, everything. I felt really stupid. And afraid."

After a few seconds, Lisa asks, "Okay, where's the receipt?"

Alan shakes his head. "I paid cash and the receipt was in the bag."

"Let's go to the store and talk to the salesperson. I'm sure they'll remember or have records or something."

Muscles twitch along Alan's jawbone. "Why do I have to prove anything?" he demands. "If you really love me, you won't need proof." He's standing now, hands clenched, his breathing once more harsh and ragged.

Lisa stammers out, "I do believe you. At least, I want to." She stands opposite him, trying to hide the panic that's welling inside. His face is twisting into a mask of rage. "I know," she says, trying to sound bright and encouraging. "If it's the stress, why don't you quit working downstairs? Move up here or back to the company?"

"I can't," he says, his voice a howl. "I have to see this through. We need the money."

"We don't need the money this badly. We're doing fine. I just want our life back the way it was." She reaches for his arm but he shakes her off.

"You may be doing fine," he snarls, "but I can't face those self-righteous bastards knowing that I failed. I have to succeed."

A peculiar mixture of pleading, rage and despair dances across his face. "If you're there for me, I can do it. I know I can. But I guess that's out of the question. To hell with you."

Before she can stop him, he bolts for the basement door. His feet clatter all the way down the stairs. Too late, Lisa runs after him and reaches the landing just as his office door slams shut. She doesn't hear it but she knows the dead bolt is shoved home. A breeze brushes past her, lifting her bangs in a puff of air. She shivers. The breeze is cold and rotten, saturated with the faint smell of a swamp.

Lisa turns away and closes the door behind her. Alan's fantasies are getting to her, too. She puts the phone back together and then searches through her address book. She punches in a number, misdialing twice before she gets it right.

"Hello?"

"Marjorie?" Lisa asks. "It's Lisa. Lisa Wilcox." She listens and then, "Uh-huh. Too long. Uh-huh. What are you doing for lunch tomorrow?"

20.

Lisa sits across from Marjorie Lanier, amazed as always. Marjorie is a tall, elegant woman whose vivid make-up, severely tailored suit and daunting intelligence should make her intimidating. But she isn't. Her strongest virtue, compassion, offsets the other facets of her personality. This is fortunate since she's a psychotherapist specializing in stress-related disorders. As Alan spouted his fantastic theories, Lisa thought of Marjorie. If anyone could help, she could. Now, sitting across from her at The Potting Shed, Lisa feels guilty. She really likes Marjorie and should have called before now. Of course, phones go both ways and Marjorie hadn't called either.

"After he proposed, I told him that even though he felt I'd saved his life, I didn't think it was the right foundation for a permanent relationship. As a result, I said no," Marjorie says, finishing the story with a good-natured laugh.

Lisa imagines this heart-broken patient moping for the rest of his life; his one true love kept from him. "What did he do then?"

"He married a blond bombshell he met in Vegas and went on a two month cruise on the Mediterranean." Rolling her eyes, she adds, "I'm sure it was to hide his deep despair."

Lisa laughs again.

"So what's going on with you?" Marjorie asks, manicured fingers wrapped around a glass of Chardonnay. Her salad and soup are mostly untouched and likely to stay that way.

"Not a whole lot," Lisa says, biting her lower lip. Now is the perfect time to explain why she asked Marjorie to lunch, but she can't. Instead, she talks about inconsequential happenings at work. Somehow, she's not sure how or why, Lisa talks about her miscarriage.

"I'm sorry," Marjorie says, shuffling greens around on her plate. "How are you feeling?"

"Mentally or physically?" Lisa asks, trying to keep her voice light, but not succeeding.

"Both."

"I don't know. One minute Alan and I are picking out strollers, the next, nothing." She feels tears building and ignores them.

Marjorie reaches across the table and gives Lisa's hand a quick squeeze. Then she drains her glass and motions to the waiter. The glass whisks away and is replaced by another. Another deep swallow and she says, "You know that's why Richard and I got a divorce, right?"

"No, I didn't." A giant fist closes around Lisa's lungs, squishing out the air.

"Both of us wanted a family, but I wanted a career first. Richard agreed, but when I was finally ready, it was too late. I had three miscarriages before I gave up. He never got over it and eventually left me." Marjorie laughs bitterly. "He then married a homely underachiever and they now have three mewling brats in a little suburban paradise." The rest of the wine is tossed back in one gulp.

"How old were you when you started trying?"

"Thirty-six. I quit at forty."

Suddenly, time is an evil, crouching beast; perfect companion for the fear that lurks in her brain. Lisa shakes her head. *Time. There has to be enough time. Alan has to get better.*

As if reading her thoughts, Marjorie says, "Speaking of significant others, how's Alan? Still cuddly as ever?"

"Still cuddly. He's actually why I called you." Lisa can't meet Marjorie's eyes, which are now intense, as if studying a lab specimen. Lisa stumbles on. "Alan started working at home about six months ago and he's starting to act strange. I'm worried."

"Uh-huh." Meaningless syllables, but encouraging somehow.

"He's been going on about evil creatures invading the basement and it's scaring me."

Marjorie sighs and pushes her salad around some more. Lisa

stifles an urge to snatch the fork away and says, "Look, Marjorie, I wanted to see you, I did. It's just that Alan is acting so strange and I don't know what to do. Don't know who to talk to. I know this is an imposition, but…"

A gentle smile plays across the therapist's lips. Bright, vampish lips. She pats Lisa's hand. "I'm not upset honey, I just can't help you."

Lisa starts to protest and Marjorie puts a finger across her own lips and says "Shhh… I can't help you, but I can help Alan." She hands Lisa a card. "Tell Alan to make an appointment. My schedule is packed, but for you kids, I'll make room."

"I—I don't know how to thank you, I…" Lisa can't continue. Her throat closes and a tear trickles down her cheek.

"It's okay. Everybody wants—needs—help these days. Luckily, I can provide it." She motions to the waiter to bring the checks and takes both.

"No," Lisa protests. "Let me get this. I mean it."

"Oh, you'll get it. You haven't seen my fees yet," Marjorie says with a grin. "For now, it's a tax write-off."

Lisa grins back and feels hope.

Back at home, Lisa examines Marjorie's business card, scanning the raised lettering: Dr. Marjorie Lanier, Ph.D. Underneath is the address of a suite in a building downtown and a phone number, but nothing else. She tucks it into one of the pigeonholes over the kitchen desk and sorts the mail.

Three envelopes catch her eye. Tensing, she reads the return addresses: 'Bug-B-Gone', 'A- Bug Solution' and 'Pest Ridders'. The dates are from last week and they contain invoices from fifty dollars to three hundred. "Alan, sweetheart, what is going on?" she murmurs. She considers confronting him, but decides against it. He needs help, that's obvious, and screaming at him isn't the answer. Sighing, she goes upstairs to change.

Lisa is in sweats and looking for her sneakers when she feels a presence in the room. She freezes, unwilling to turn around and see what has followed her into the bedroom. *Is Alan right after all? Has the evil ventured out of the basement?* Her heart hammers in her chest and she shrieks as a hand lands on her shoulder. She whirls around and faces Alan. He is glaring, a white business card in his hand.

Laughing shakily, Lisa wills her heart to slow down. "You scared me to death," she says. Alan remains frozen, his face clouded with anger. "Alan? What's wrong?"

"What's this?" he asks, his face neutral.

"Where'd you get that?"

"In the desk, where you hid it."

Lisa bites her lower lip. "I wasn't hiding it. It's from a friend. We had lunch today."

"The shrink?"

"Actually she's a psychotherapist," Lisa corrects.

"Whatever," Alan snaps. "So what did you talk about at lunch? Huh? Me, maybe?"

Lisa cringes and swallows, hard.

Alan's eyes narrow to slits. "You think I'm crazy, don't you?" He glares at her, nostrils flaring in and out, the now typical brick-red flush suffusing his face. "Don't you?" he screams.

Fear, concern, anger, love fight for control. Anger wins. "Shouldn't I?" she demands. "Just how many exterminators have you called? Have they found anything? Anything at all? Or are they just taking your—our—money and laughing all the way to the bank?"

Alan steps back, his eyes darting left to right, never meeting hers. "There's something there," he mutters, "and it's getting stronger."

Lisa's anger collapses. "Alan," she says and touches his arm. He pulls back, glaring at the spot where she touched him. A dull ache wells up. "Sweetheart, please, just talk to Marjorie. She specializes in—in cases like yours. She can help."

"Cases like mine? You mean nutcases? Psychos?" He brays a harsh laugh. "Unless she's got a flame thrower or industrial strength rat traps, there's not a whole lot she can do."

Desperate, Lisa tries again. "Alan, there's nothing there.

Maybe talking about what's going on will—"

Alan grabs her by the shoulders and thrusts his face close to hers. "Talking about it will do NOTHING. There is something in the basement and it is DANGEROUS." He releases her and she falls on the bed. He points his finger at her and says, "And you. Stop dissecting me with your friends. I can handle this," he says and stomps out of the room.

After a short silence, Lisa hears the kitchen door slam. With a gasp, she releases the air in her lungs, unaware that she's been holding her breath. She sits in stunned silence, but doesn't cry.

21.

It's hard to tell how long the doorbell has been ringing. In the back of her mind, she thinks it has been some time. When she pulls open the front door Steve is framed in the opening, fist upraised to start banging. "It's about time…" he begins but Lisa cuts him off.

"You're lucky I answered at all," she snaps and walks towards the kitchen. Steve catches up with her and spins her around.

"Lisa, what's going on?"

"I don't know, Steve. I just don't know," she says and rubs her forehead with her eyes closed. His arms close around her and she leans against him, grateful for his strong presence. She pulls back and tries a small smile. It doesn't feel too bad. "Beer?"

"That'd be great," Steve says and follows her into the kitchen. Once they each have a bottle, he asks, "What's for dinner? Or is this it?"

Lisa frowns, her eyebrows knitted together. "Dinner?"

"Uh-huh. Listen, are you guys trying to tell me something? This is the second time we've misconnected on the dinner thing."

"No," Lisa says, her expression finally softening. "If we wanted to get rid of you we'd just say so. Unfortunately, I forgot again. Alan and I had a fight and everything else just went out the window." A shiver runs down her back and she takes a big swallow of beer.

"Where is the big guy?"

"Entrenched in his fortress," she says, the bitterness causing Steve's eyebrows to rise. He studies her.

"That bad, huh?"

"That bad."

"Then let's go roust him," Steve says as he grabs Lisa's hand and pulls her towards the basement.

Steve tromps down the stairs. Lisa follows, but hesitates on the landing, afraid to descend into the dim recesses. Steve pauses halfway and turns. "What's wrong?"

"I have a funny feeling," Lisa stammers. "Do you smell something—bad?"

"You mean the dampness?" Steve asks, his voice puzzled.

Lisa wants to scream. Instead, she nods, her eyes feeling ten times their normal size.

Steve shrugs. "It was a wet winter. There's a leak somewhere. The house is still under warranty, isn't it?"

Lisa nods again; unable to talk around the lump in her throat.

"Get your builder to come out and take a look. Now, come on," he says, motioning for her to join him.

Taking a deep breath, Lisa clutches at the offered hand and follows him the rest of the way. Resisting only a little.

At the bottom, Steve glances around and gives a low whistle. "What's all this?" he asks and picks up a flashlight, one of a half dozen to the right of the stairs.

Lisa frowns. "I'm not sure; they weren't here last week." She pauses, scanning the concrete floor. "Here's more," she says and points to another couple of dozen scattered between the stairs and the office door.

"Lisa," Steve says, his brown eyes black in the gloom. "We need to get Alan out of here."

"I couldn't agree more. But it's not going to be easy."

While she's talking, Steve moves to the door. Banging as loud as he can, he yells, "Alan, it's me, Steve." He stops and listens.

Lisa feels her heart slam against her chest. Nothing.

Steve tries again, hitting the door harder, "Alan, open up." Still nothing.

Lisa's shoulders slump. "Let's go," she says, touching his arm. "We can call him from the kitchen."

"Wait," Steve says and Lisa stops. "These flashlights are dangerous. In the dark, someone could step on one and go flying."

Lisa agrees. She locates an empty box and they gather the

lights, pushing the box against the wall when it's full. This time, she leads the way up the stairs and he follows, occasionally looking back over his shoulder at the mute door.

Alan sprawls on the couch clutching a half-empty beer bottle in one hand. Five empty ones are scattered on the floor in front of him. A movie he's seen often enough to have the script memorized fills the television screen. Blearily, he watches it again, voicing the dialogue before the characters. The combination of alcohol and boredom is making his eyelids droop. He doesn't mind. Sleep—oblivion—keeps him from thinking about the unfinished project, the creatures outside, and, most of all, Lisa. Just as he is about to slide into unconsciousness, the phone shrills, jerking him back to life.

The phone rings once before voicemail kicks in. Alan listens for the chirp that says a message has arrived. When it does, he picks up the phone and listens, tensing, as a familiar voice flows from the device.

"Hey, big guy, did you forget our dinner date?" Steve asks. "I'm feeling unwanted."

Alan finishes his beer in one swallow, wincing at the flatness. Steve continues. "Here's somebody that misses you more than me."

Mild protestations are heard in the background and then Lisa is on the line. "Alan, sweetheart, please come up and have dinner with us." A pause and he can hear low whispers, but not loud enough to make out. "It's not nice to ignore your friends. Or your wife."

The phone is silent and then Steve is back. "Okay, maybe you're in the bathroom or something. Anyway, I'm here and would really like to talk to you. Come up when you can." There's a click and then silence.

Frozen for a few seconds, Alan scowls and flings his bottle across the room. It hooks to the right and shatters against his desk. "Nobody tells me what to do," he yells. The air is hot and close and bright flashes of light blossom. He closes his eyes and sinks into the couch, his throbbing head cradled in his hands.

Alan is overcome by a deep weariness. He stretches out on the couch and slips into nothingness while the television blares on.

"That was certainly productive," Steve says, his mouth twisted in a wry grimace.

"At least we tried," Lisa assures him. Then she frowns. "I haven't tried for a long time. A really long time. This is my fault."

Steve puts his arm around her and gives a quick squeeze. "What's important right now is to get him back among the land of the living."

His concern makes her feel better and she moves towards the pantry. "Let's whip up some dinner. How does spaghetti sound?"

"Great," Steve says, pitching in. "I'll still feel neglected but I won't be hungry."

Lisa grins. "Don't be so sure. You haven't tasted my cooking yet." Soon the kitchen bubbles with the spicy aroma of tomatoes and herbs.

Their loaded plates are carried into the family room along with a bottle of wine and three glasses. Lisa still hopes Alan will come upstairs even though the prospect is looking grim. The two spread out in front of the fireplace, their backs propped against the couch. The savory sauce belies Lisa's protestations and it's a few minutes before either stop eating long enough to talk.

Steve speaks first. "I have a confession," he says, sipping his wine.

With a grin, Lisa asks, "Is it juicy?"

"Unfortunately no," Steve admits.

The grin fades when she sees his expression. "What is it?"

"I didn't come over just to see you guys. I came to check up on Alan and see why he postponed the design review."

Lisa scowls. "He postponed it? Why?"

"He said he wasn't ready. Personal reasons."

"That's ridiculous," she bursts out. She takes a deep breath. "What I mean is, he's down there all the time. If he's not working on his project, what the hell is he doing?"

"I don't know," Steve says. "I haven't talked to him in weeks. I've been preoccupied and I guess it just got away from me."

Lisa studies him. She can tell he's worried about Alan, but there's something else going on. "So why is this such a horrible thing to confess?"

Steve touches her hand. "Because you two are my best friends," he says, softly, "and I don't ever want to do anything to betray that friendship."

Lisa squeezes back. "Don't worry about that. Doing something because you care about Alan isn't going to upset him or me. Well, me anyway."

"What do you mean?"

"It's hard to predict how Alan is going to react." She tells him about the lunch with Marjorie and the subsequent blow-up by Alan. As she recounts the story, heat ripples across her face that has nothing to do with the fireplace.

"Why do you think Alan was so worked up over her card?"

"You don't know the half of it," Lisa says. In response to Steve's gentle prodding, she tells him everything. It comes out in a flood. Alan's obsession with the basement, the exterminators, the ferret, his isolation; everything.

Steve rubs the back of his neck. "Wow, I didn't know it's that bad. He refuses to talk to your friend?"

Lisa nods. Both sit for a few minutes. Lisa wondering how things could have gone from so high to so low in two short months and Steve sitting quietly, thinking about whatever is bothering him. Watching him reminds Lisa of an earlier comment. "You said you've been preoccupied," she says. "With what?"

The dancing flames captivate Steve, his eyes darting back and forth. Just as Lisa is about to ask him again, he says, "It's Beth. She wants to get married."

Lisa's heart hammers and she doesn't trust herself to speak.

A sip of wine steadies her nerves. She clears her throat and, as lightly as she can, says, "Really? I think that's great. It's time you settle down with somebody you love."

Abruptly, Steve stands and walks to the fire, poking at the logs and causing sparks to shimmer up the chimney. "That's just it," he says. "I don't think I love her." His movements are jerkier now, almost vicious as he stabs the blaze.

An odd feeling pours through her body. With a start, Lisa recognizes it as relief. "But you two get along so well; it's as if you were made for each other."

"That's what everybody says," Steve murmurs, as if talking to himself. "It's just that there's no spark." An embarrassed laugh. "No magic."

Lisa doesn't laugh in return. "I know what you mean. Alan and I used to have magic, but not anymore." She becomes very still. When she speaks again, it's from a distance. "I think—if it were still Alan, there would still be excitement. But it's not him anymore. I—I don't know who that is down in the basement. Maybe if there had been a baby..."

Steve stops attacking the fire and sits on the couch, pulling Lisa up beside him and draping one arm around her shoulders. She relaxes against him, breathing in the woodsy fragrance that clings to him and enjoying the way his arm feels on her shoulders. Steve rests his cheek against her head and says, "This reminds me of college."

"Mmmm," she agrees. A tear slides down her cheek. College, the three of them, everything that belonged to that life is an eternity ago. Back then, anything and everything was possible. She wipes a tear away with the back of her hand.

"She wants kids," Steve announces, his voice drab.

Yanked back to the present, Lisa asks, "Who?"

"Beth," he says, pulling back slightly so he can look at her. "Have you heard anything?"

"Of course I have." Lisa punches him lightly and then moves so she can see his face. "What do *you* want?"

Steve's eyes bore into hers. "You."

22.

Groaning, Alan struggles to an upright position and jabs at the remote to stop the television's mindless drivel. The abrupt silence echoes around the room, but his head continues to pound. He rubs his temples, but it's useless. Staggering to the bathroom, he yanks open the medicine cabinet. The green aspirin bottle glows like a beacon and he clutches at it, succor at hand. Four white tablets fall out of the bottle and are quickly tossed back. The acrid taste cuts through his grogginess and he waits for the aspirin to take effect. A haggard image with bloodshot eyes stares out from the vanity mirror.

"My god," Alan says to the hideous stranger. "No wonder Lisa screamed when she saw me. What have I done?" He contemplates the almost unrecognizable visage then says, "What am I doing?"

The pain fades and Alan blinks slowly, the muscles behind his eyes flexing with newfound ease. He walks into the main room and is shocked by what he sees.

Typically neat, almost to obsession, Alan had quit caring about his surroundings. Trash spills out of plastic bags, flies circling over them in lazy patterns. A sickly sweet smell permeates the room and empty beer bottles are strewn carelessly over the floor. Alan wipes his perspiring forehead with the back of a sticky hand. He focuses on the filth-encrusted hand and its fingernails, caked with dirt. Alan shudders, not wanting to believe they are really his, but unable to deny it. Shocked by his own degradation, he stumbles through the room, cataloguing each example of bestiality. Halfway across the room, he can't take it any longer and leans over a chair and retches, clearing his stomach of beer and junk.

Alan straightens up, his head as clear as his stomach. Now he looks around the room, seeing not the depths that he's sunk to, but what it will take to get back. *Lisa's right. Maybe I should make an appointment with her friend.* Until he can talk to her, though, he needs to improve some things himself. A shower is first and back to work next. The project is behind but not unsalvageable. Feeling as if he's stepped back from the abyss, Alan moves towards the bathroom, but stops when he sees the cell phone. He remembers Lisa and Steve begging him to come upstairs. But not like this. Guilt marching through his head, he shaves, takes a quick shower and changes into clean clothes. Almost presentable, he walks to the door, broken glass crunching underfoot.

He throws open the door, but then hesitates as he stares into the eerie space, lit by the dim light of the treacherous fluorescent bulb. The room is quiet, but Alan knows that won't last. His nerves tingle, the silence more terrifying than any din. At least when the creatures make noise he knows where they are. Now they could be anywhere. He swallows, his throat tight against the fear that erupts from his stomach.

Alan stands, his shadow stretching into the darkness, deciding what to do. A black shadow skitters past him on the right and disappears into his office. He whirls around, but it's gone. Just beyond his peripheral vision, another shape flicks into what has been his sanctuary. Feeling dizzy, he wheels to that side, again just missing whatever made the movement. His tongue darts out, sticking against parched, cracked lips. He scans the room, registering nothing, but knowing something is there. He eases the door shut, leaning against it as it clicks home. Shakily, he turns the dead bolt. The loud 'snick' reverberates against the walls. Bile rises and he gulps it down, forbidding his body to turn against him.

Constantly scanning the area, Alan moves stealthily towards the phone. He's never known the creatures to come out when there's more than one person around. Steve will come and help him out—out of this trap.

The journey to the phone is tense but uneventful. Not taking his eyes off potential danger spots, Alan turns his back to the wall and watches the shadows along the opposite walls while he gropes blindly for his phone. Its smooth curve makes him want to weep in gratitude as he curls his fingers around it. Just as he picks it up, a searing pain twists through his hand and the phone falls to the floor, shattering.

Yelping, Alan wheels around in time to see a scorpion-like tail disappear behind the desk. A welt with an angry red dot in the center is rising on his hand. Fire spreads from the sting in ever widening circles. Alan brings his hand to his mouth and sucks the wound, easing the pain. As quickly as he puts it in his mouth, he jerks it away; spitting out the acrid taste that fills his mouth. His tongue grows numb and he wonders how lethal the poison is.

Frantically, he looks around his prison for an escape route. The only exit other than the door is the walled up window. And, thanks to the soundproofing and the smashed phone, there's no way to contact anyone. Like it or not, the only way out is through the basement.

Lisa stares at Steve, her heart thundering in her ears. She drinks deeply from her glass, almost choking on the wine. Steve reaches for her hand. "Did you hear what I said?" he asks, like a schoolboy admitting a crush.

"Uh-huh." With a shaky laugh, she adds, "Not sure I believe it, though."

"You don't have to. I do."

Before she can stop him, he leans over and kisses her hard and deep, drinking from the depths of her soul. Just when Lisa thinks she is going to pass out, he pulls back and releases her, leaving her dizzy. Steve walks to the window and stares out into the bleak February night. Lisa joins him at the window, not saying anything, content to let him talk first.

When he does speak, his voice is ragged, harsh with suppressed emotion. "I'm sorry. I-I've always loved you but never said anything because you were happy. Because Alan made you happy. But now, it's all wrong. He's my best friend, but you deserve better. You deserve me."

Lisa doesn't know what to say. What to feel. And so she says nothing. Just stands beside Steve and looks out into February while the fire dances and glows and rain drums a soothing tattoo on the window.

Alan stands by the desk, measuring the distance to the door and sweeping the room for—things... Even though the only sounds he hears are his lungs and heart beating against each other, he knows the creatures are here. But where? Moving slowly, putting each foot down carefully, deliberately, he inches towards the door. Once outside, he's sure he can beat them to the stairs. *I've done it before*, he thinks, glancing at the three scars running down his arm. *I can do it again.* Steadily, he gains on freedom.

The distance is shrinking, but slowly. Far too slowly. He walks faster and suddenly the air is full of screeching bats. But they're not bats. The creatures have leathery wings and short, furry bodies, but that's where the resemblance ends. The fliers have fangs that drip thick ooze and scorpion tails whip out behind them. One zips close to Alan's face and catches his cheek with the razor sharp point. He shrieks and claps a hand to the angry welt left behind. It's identical to the one on his hand, only magnitudes more painful. As if on cue, a cloud of the beasts fly at Alan, attacking with claws and tails. He shields his face as best he can but the creatures slice into his flesh, laying open unprotected skin.

Fighting desperately to get away, Alan whirls and swings his arms, flinging putrid bodies across the room, only to have more replace them. Out of the swarm, a creature larger than the rest soars upward. With a loud explosion and a shower of glass, it hits the light bulb, plunging the room into darkness.

The sudden absence of light shocks everything into immobility. Alan recovers first and runs. As he moves towards the door, his ankle is slashed. Screaming, he collapses onto the floor, hands outstretched to stop his fall. They hit unyielding glass. Shards from the broken light bulb and beer bottles slice into soft tissue, magnifying his agony. Still screaming, he scrambles across the floor, his knees and palms lacerated by the razor-like glass. As he crawls, the evil beasts attack; stinging, biting, clawing. His body becomes numb under the steady onslaught of pain and poison.

Alan's screams decrease to a low, constant moan and his entire universe collapses to the single goal of reaching the door. The blackness is absolute but the creatures still find him. Just as he is about to give in to their ceaseless attack, his head smacks the doorframe. Sobbing, he pulls himself up and wrenches the door open.

Lisa slowly opens her eyes, disoriented by too much wine and too little sleep. The fire is out, leaving the room damp and chilly. She shivers, and the movement wakens Steve. He smiles, holding back a yawn.

"Hey, sleepy head," he says and gives her a hug and a quick kiss on the top of her head.

She pulls away and his smile disappears. Snapshots of the evening click through her brain. The kiss. The confession. Another kiss. Wine. More kisses. More wine. And then...

"I don't—I can't—remember..." She stutters, feeling sick and not just from the wine.

His eyes soften and the smile is back. "We just kissed. You're a good woman and I'm a bad friend."

"We just kissed?"

"Yeah, and you cried. And I tried to talk you into more. And you cried some more." His smile is crooked, sheepish. "I'm glad you're true to Alan. But I'm not giving up."

"You understand that regardless of how I feel about you, I can never do anything to hurt Alan, right?"

"How *do* you feel about me?" Steve asks, his head cocked and his eyes blazing.

Lisa drops her eyes, her voice low, almost incomprehensible. "I love you, too."

Steve nods; his face solemn. "That's enough for now. But I can't marry Beth and let her plan some fantasy life when it's you that I love. I couldn't before and I can't now. I just can't," he adds vehemently.

"I'm sorry," she whispers, tears threatening again.

Steve hugs her, enveloping her in the heady scent of wood

smoke and his own spicy fragrance. Traitorously, her body arches to his, aching to feel more, wanting to give in to their overwhelming need. Abruptly, she pulls back, pushing him away and trying to catch her breath. Pain and understanding battle on Steve's face as he stands up and walks away, looking for his coat. Lisa watches him, unable to say anything more.

He stops at the door. "I'm calling Beth when I get home."

"It's late," Lisa says.

"True, but it's only going to get later."

She nods and tries to smile, leaning against the open door. Steve gives her a quick kiss on the cheek and strides out into the cold, cloudy night. Lisa eases the door shut and runs up the stairs.

Once upstairs, she drops onto the bed and takes a deep breath, holding it until bright spots of light dance against her eyelids. It rushes out in a loud 'whoosh' and she cries. Lisa cries for the baby that never was, she cries for Alan, for Steve, and mostly she cries for what she's lost—and gained—tonight. She falls asleep, still sobbing in her dreams.

Outside on the sidewalk, Steve pauses and looks back towards the house. The basement windows are dark, a gloomy contrast to the warm light streaming from the upstairs bedroom. The more he contemplates the two, the more his anger grows. *Alan is my friend. I have to make him understand what he's doing. What he's losing.* Breathing quick and shallow, heart pounding in his chest, Steve heads back to the house.

Alan slaps the foul creatures off him as he steps out into the basement. Above his thundering heart, he hears a cacophony. Horrible slitherings and claws that click and skitter. Overhead, leathery wings swoop, accompanied by the hissing he knows too well. The light is out and he looks for the flashlights, but they're gone. He can feel his already rapid heartbeat crank up a notch as thoughts race through his head. *Are they intelligent? Did they hide the flashlights?* Just then, the moon peeks out from leaden clouds and dimly lights the open space. Renewed hope somewhat calms the hammering in his chest and Alan readies for the final dash. His wounds are numb with spreading poison, but a new pain has appeared. Each ragged breath he pulls in, every beat of his exhausted heart produces fresh agony. Gasping, he staggers across the basement floor to the sanctity of the stairs.

Halfway to his goal, the moon completely emerges from the clouds and brightly illuminates the basement. Every square inch is covered with writhing, mewling creatures, some with stingers, others with claws and fangs, and all with flat, merciless eyes. The pain in Alan's chest escalates and he stumbles, falling face down onto the cold, unforgiving concrete. The creatures pour off the wall, flying, crawling, sliding; all focused on the helpless man. He rolls over in time to see the horde descending. As he opens his mouth to scream, a slime-encrusted monstrosity flies into his mouth. He yanks it out and uses it as a club to beat off its brethren. By moonlight he sees the stairs, blessedly clear, and makes a final dash for freedom.

The trip to the top is a blur and he reaches the landing seconds ahead of the now regrouped mass. He clutches at the door knob and can't find purchase; his hands are covered in slime. Grasping tendrils caress his legs and tickle his lower back. Almost lovingly. Sure of its prize. Alan flails against the unyielding door, sobbing with exhaustion and pain. Suddenly, the door bursts open and he falls into the kitchen.

"Alan, what the hell…" says Steve as he turns, his hand still on the knob.

Sprawled on the kitchen floor, Alan sees the menacing horde hesitating at the light. He watches as hideous feelers creep out of the darkness and encircle Steve's ankles. Confused, his friend looks down and, before Alan can warn him, the monstrosity tightens and yanks. Shrieking, Steve is dragged backward, his hand still clutching the door. It slams, cutting short an inhuman howl. The only sounds drifting from behind the door are that of a contented feeding.

Epilogue

Elizabeth—Liz—loves the new neighborhood. And her new neighbors. She smiles at Amy across the table.

"I'm so glad you two bought this house," Amy bubbles, sipping her coffee.

"Me too," Liz agrees. "We got a great deal."

Amy nods. "The Sub-Prime Fiasco?"

"No. It was a foreclosure, but a lot sadder than just not being able to pay bills..."

"How so?" Amy asks and puts down her coffee.

"Kind of freaky, actually," Liz says with a frown. "Some guy, I think a friend of the owners, fell down the basement stairs and broke his neck. Then, the owner had a heart-attack and died the same night."

Amy stares.

"The wife had some kind of breakdown and had to sell the house to pay for medical bills," Liz finishes and picks up her cup, cradling it and inhaling the fragrance.

Amy shakes her head and continues to stare. "How can you live in this house? Negative energy has a way of hanging around."

Liz laughs and it's a tinny, hollow laugh that bounces around the kitchen. "You make your own energy. Besides, have you seen the suite downstairs? It'll make a great office for my catering business. It was the selling point of the house. Well, that and the price."

"I don't know," Amy says. "I still think it's really creepy."

"Nothing creeps me out. Especially when there's equity to be had. Except maybe rats." Liz pauses. "Can you recommend a good exterminator? I've been hearing noises in the basement. I think we've got varmints."